Disney

Tangled

THE STORY OF THE MOVIE IN COMICS

DARK HORSE BOOKS

Once upon a time, a single drop of sunlight fell from the heavens.

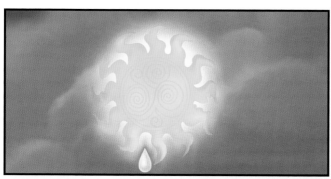

FROM THIS SMALL DROP OF SUN...

...GREW A **MAGICAL GOLDEN FLOWER**, WITH THE POWER TO HEAL THE SICK AND INJURIED.

NEARBY, WAS A GLORIOUS KINGDOM.

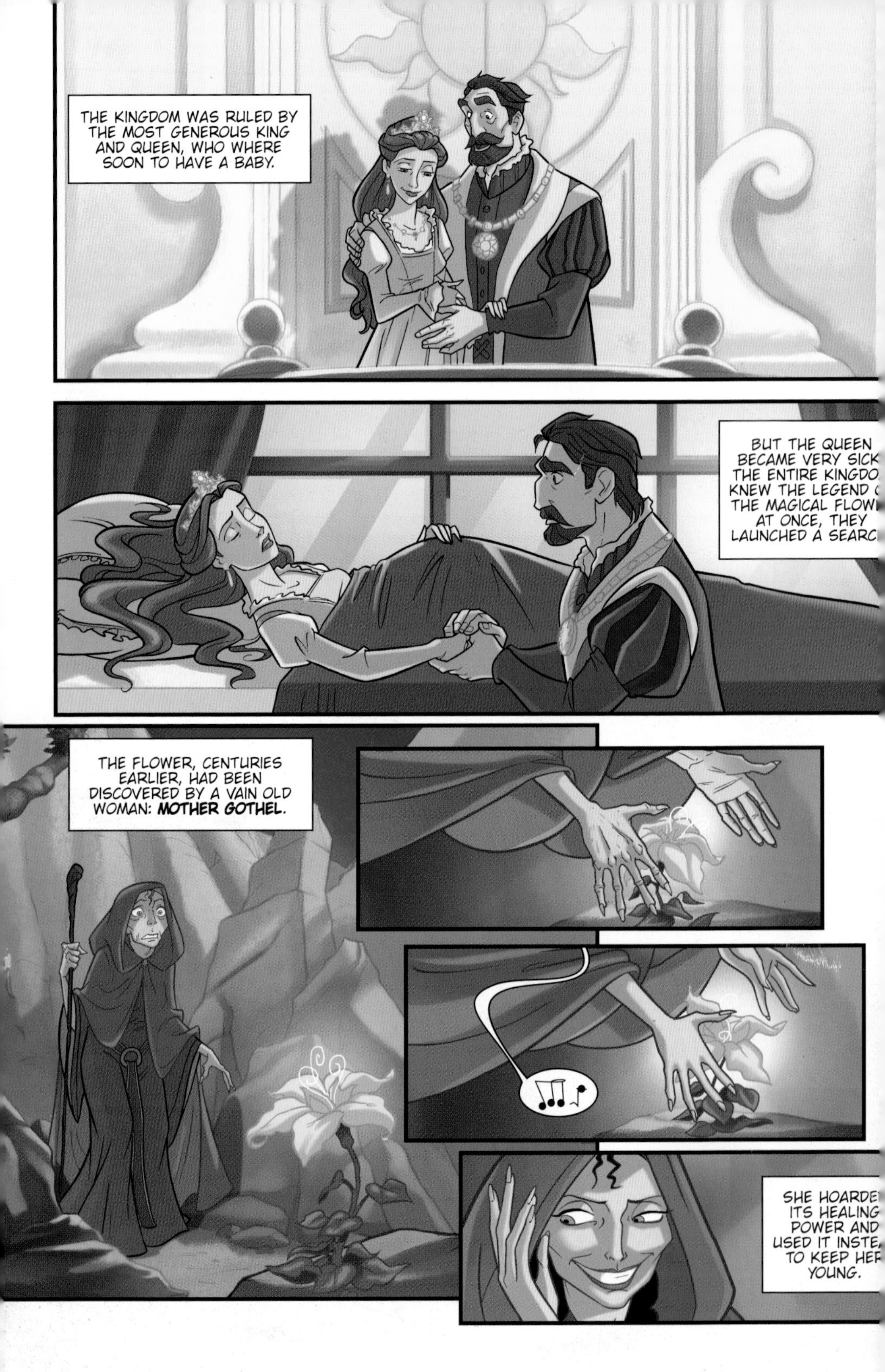
THE KINGDOM WAS RULED BY THE MOST GENEROUS KING AND QUEEN, WHO WHERE SOON TO HAVE A BABY.
BUT THE QUEEN BECAME VERY SICK THE ENTIRE KINGDO KNEW THE LEGEND THE MAGICAL FLOW AT ONCE, THEY LAUNCHED A SEARC
THE FLOWER, CENTURIES EARLIER, HAD BEEN DISCOVERED BY A VAIN OLD WOMAN: MOTHER GOTHEL.
SHE HOARDE ITS HEALING POWER AND USED IT INSTE TO KEEP HER YOUNG.

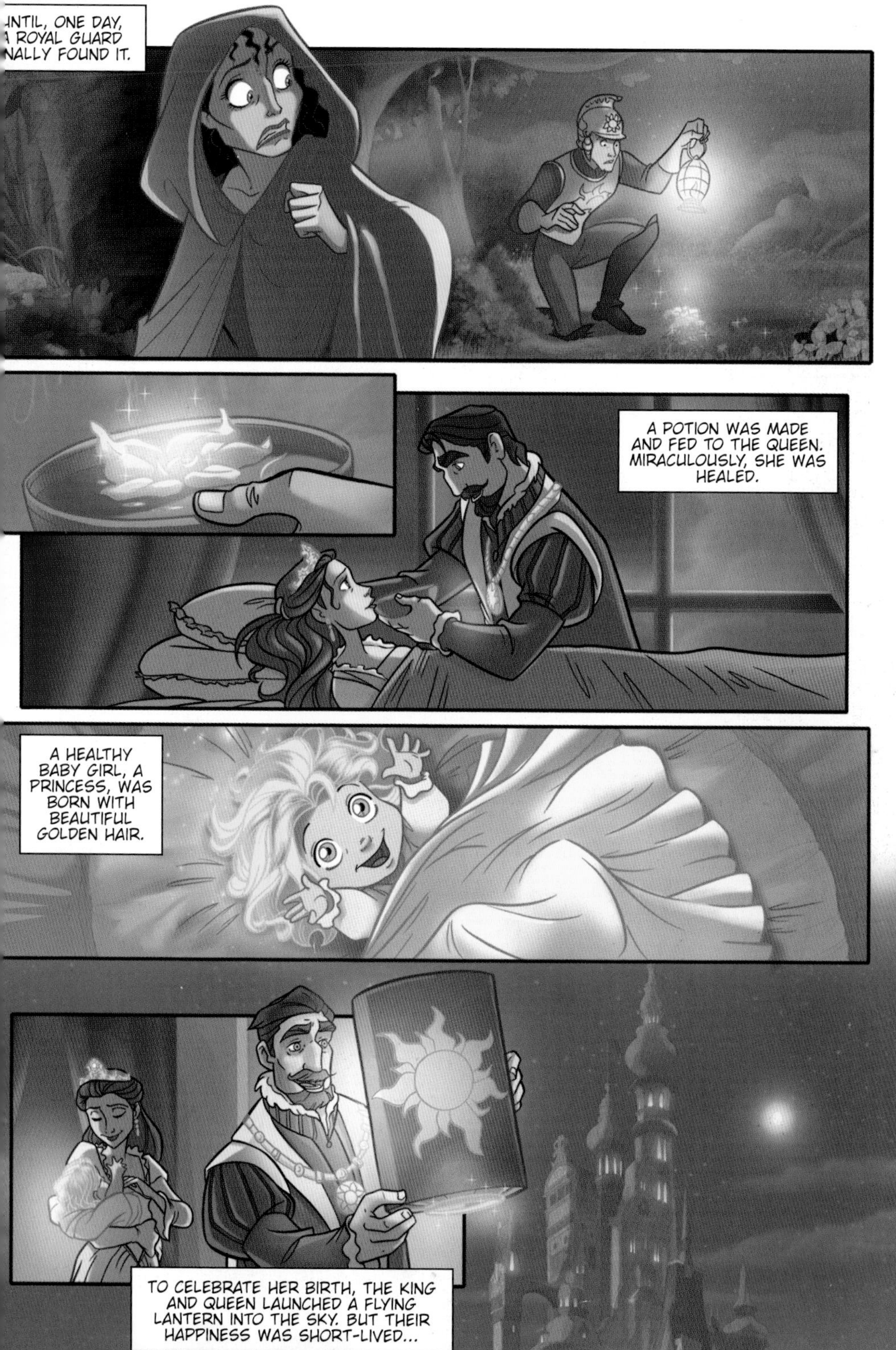
NTIL, ONE DAY, A ROYAL GUARD NALLY FOUND IT.
A POTION WAS MADE AND FED TO THE QUEEN. MIRACULOUSLY, SHE WAS HEALED.
A HEALTHY BABY GIRL, A PRINCESS, WAS BORN WITH BEAUTIFUL GOLDEN HAIR.
TO CELEBRATE HER BIRTH, THE KING AND QUEEN LAUNCHED A FLYING LANTERN INTO THE SKY. BUT THEIR HAPPINESS WAS SHORT-LIVED...

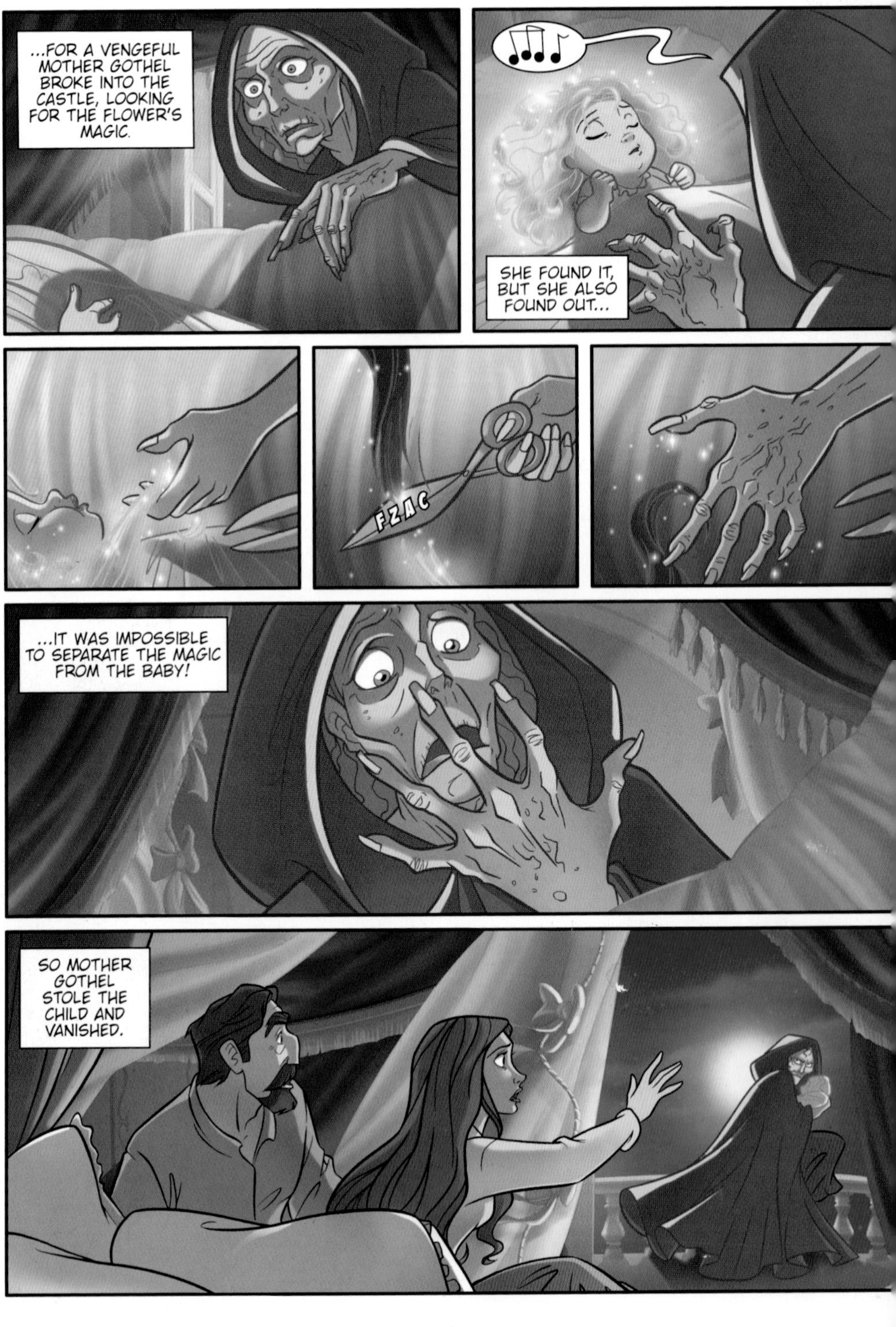
...FOR A VENGEFUL MOTHER GOTHEL BROKE INTO THE CASTLE, LOOKING FOR THE FLOWER'S MAGIC.
SHE FOUND IT, BUT SHE ALSO FOUND OUT...
FZAC
...IT WAS IMPOSSIBLE TO SEPARATE THE MAGIC FROM THE BABY!
SO MOTHER GOTHEL STOLE THE CHILD AND VANISHED.

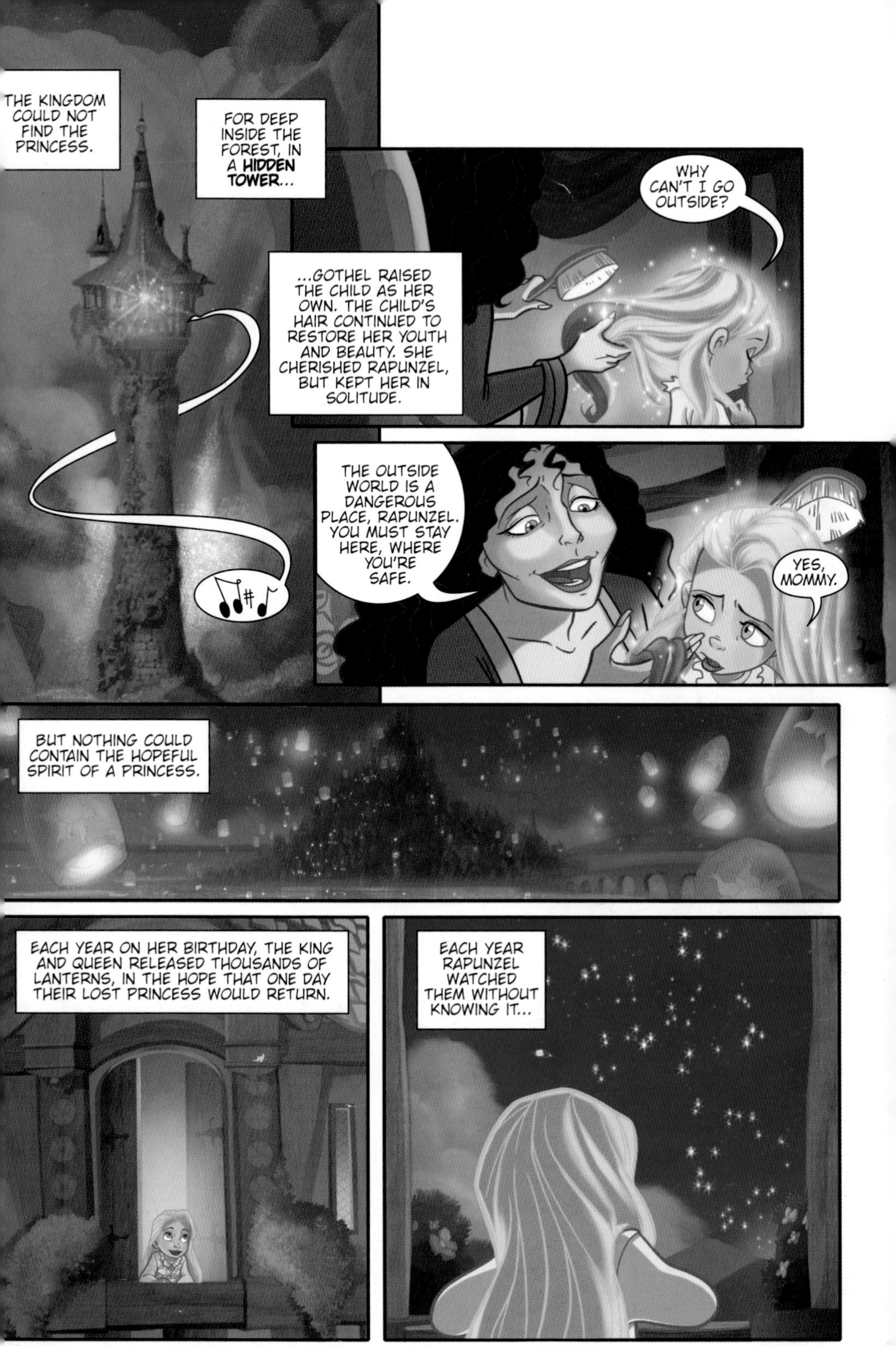
THE KINGDOM COULD NOT FIND THE PRINCESS.
FOR DEEP INSIDE THE FOREST, IN A **HIDDEN TOWER**...
...GOTHEL RAISED THE CHILD AS HER OWN. THE CHILD'S HAIR CONTINUED TO RESTORE HER YOUTH AND BEAUTY. SHE CHERISHED RAPUNZEL, BUT KEPT HER IN SOLITUDE.
WHY CAN'T I GO OUTSIDE?
THE OUTSIDE WORLD IS A DANGEROUS PLACE, RAPUNZEL. YOU MUST STAY HERE, WHERE YOU'RE SAFE.
YES, MOMMY.
BUT NOTHING COULD CONTAIN THE HOPEFUL SPIRIT OF A PRINCESS.
EACH YEAR ON HER BIRTHDAY, THE KING AND QUEEN RELEASED THOUSANDS OF LANTERNS, IN THE HOPE THAT ONE DAY THEIR LOST PRINCESS WOULD RETURN.
EACH YEAR RAPUNZEL WATCHED THEM WITHOUT KNOWING IT...

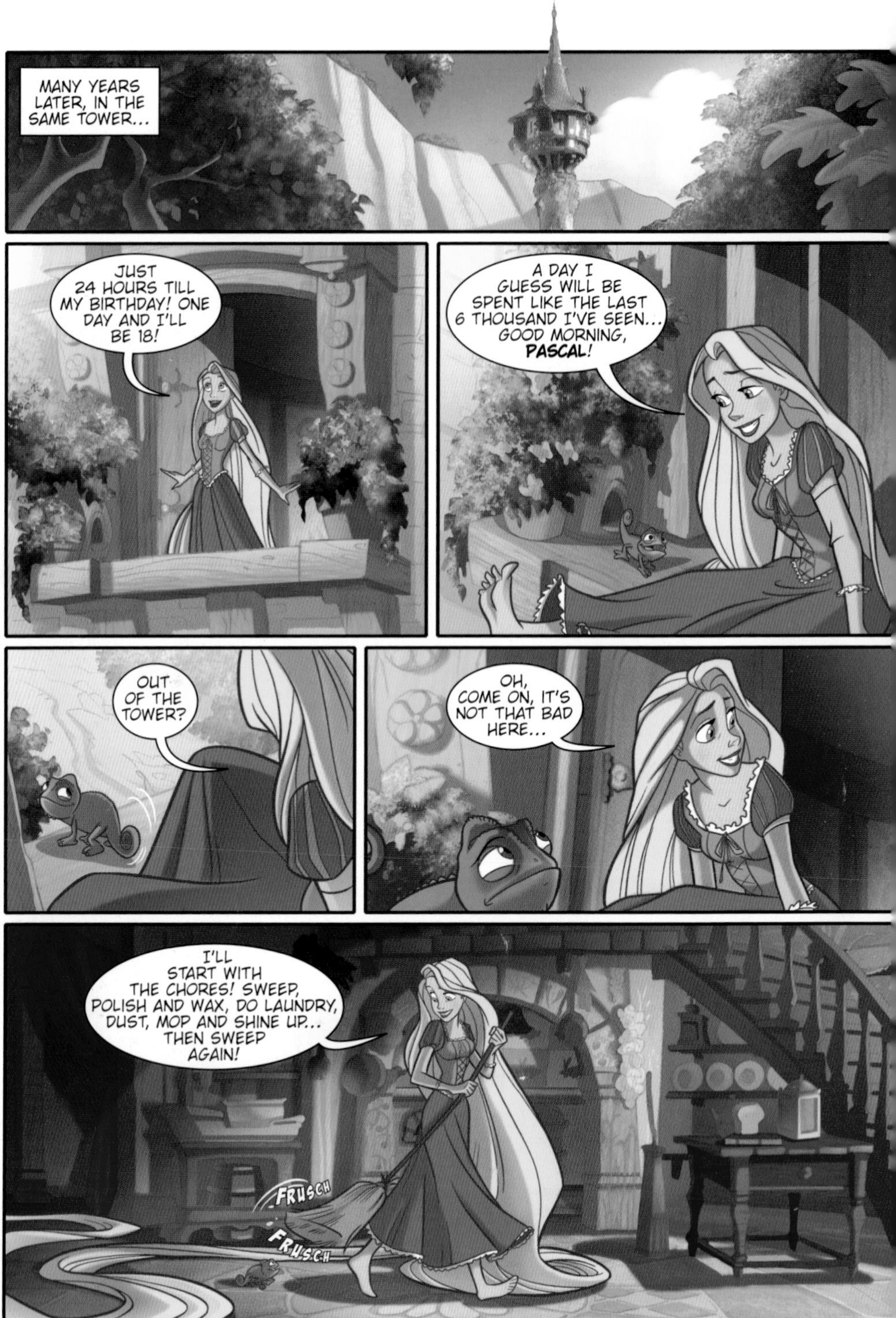
MANY YEARS LATER, IN THE SAME TOWER...
JUST 24 HOURS TILL MY BIRTHDAY! ONE DAY AND I'LL BE 18!
A DAY I GUESS WILL BE SPENT LIKE THE LAST 6 THOUSAND I'VE SEEN... GOOD MORNING, PASCAL!
OUT OF THE TOWER?
OH, COME ON, IT'S NOT THAT BAD HERE...
I'LL START WITH THE CHORES! SWEEP, POLISH AND WAX, DO LAUNDRY, DUST, MOP AND SHINE UP... THEN SWEEP AGAIN!
FRUSCH
FRUSCH

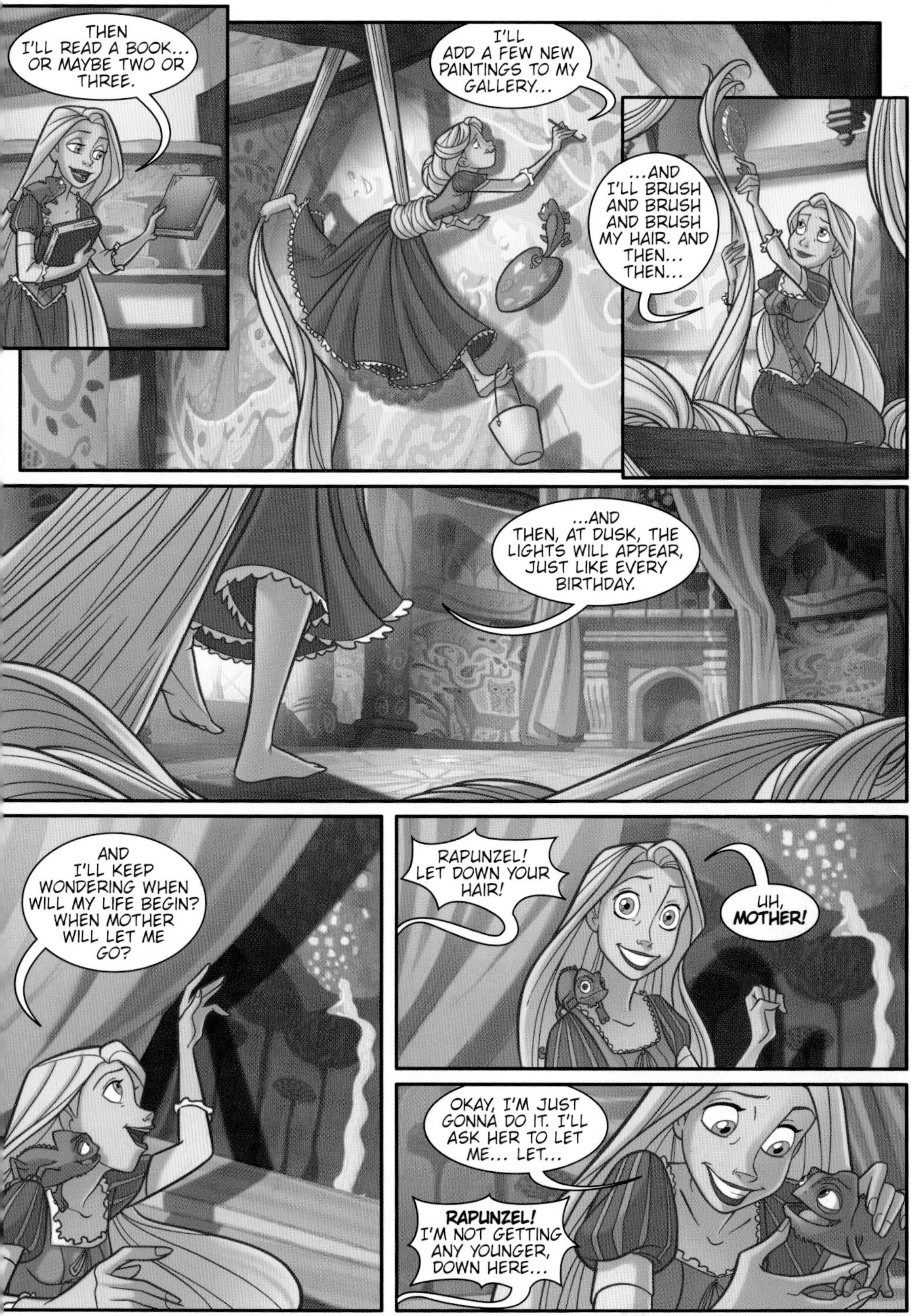

THEN I'LL READ A BOOK... OR MAYBE TWO OR THREE.
I'LL ADD A FEW NEW PAINTINGS TO MY GALLERY...
...AND I'LL BRUSH AND BRUSH AND BRUSH MY HAIR. AND THEN... THEN...
...AND THEN, AT DUSK, THE LIGHTS WILL APPEAR, JUST LIKE EVERY BIRTHDAY.
AND I'LL KEEP WONDERING WHEN WILL MY LIFE BEGIN? WHEN MOTHER WILL LET ME GO?
RAPUNZEL! LET DOWN YOUR HAIR!
UH, MOTHER!
OKAY, I'M JUST GONNA DO IT. I'LL ASK HER TO LET ME... LET...
RAPUNZEL! I'M NOT GETTING ANY YOUNGER, DOWN HERE...

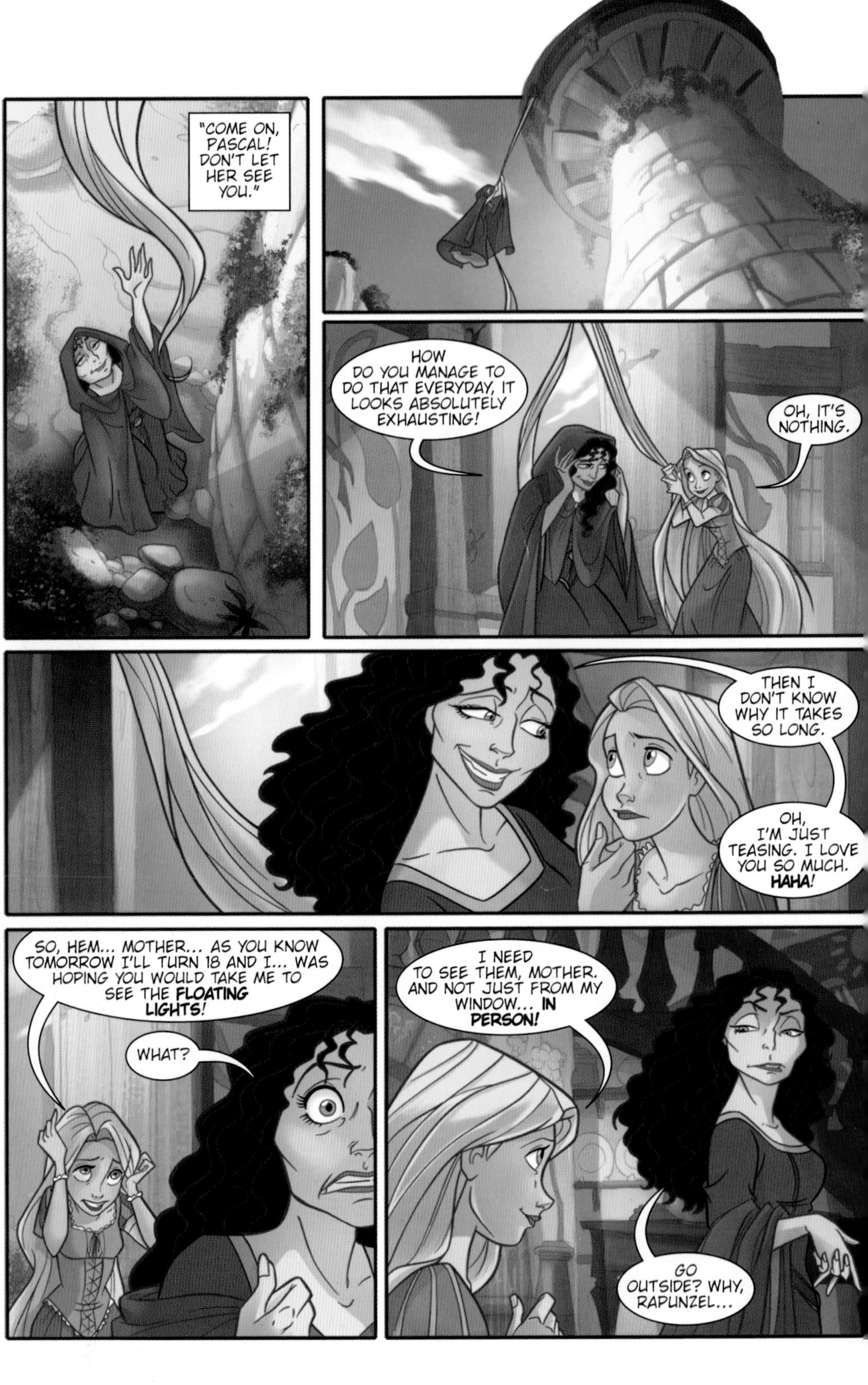
"COME ON, PASCAL! DON'T LET HER SEE YOU."
HOW DO YOU MANAGE TO DO THAT EVERYDAY, IT LOOKS ABSOLUTELY EXHAUSTING!
OH, IT'S NOTHING.
THEN I DON'T KNOW WHY IT TAKES SO LONG.
OH, I'M JUST TEASING. I LOVE YOU SO MUCH. **HAHA**!
SO, HEM... MOTHER... AS YOU KNOW TOMORROW I'LL TURN 18 AND I... WAS HOPING YOU WOULD TAKE ME TO SEE THE **FLOATING LIGHTS**!
WHAT?
I NEED TO SEE THEM, MOTHER. AND NOT JUST FROM MY WINDOW... **IN PERSON!**
GO OUTSIDE? WHY, RAPUNZEL...

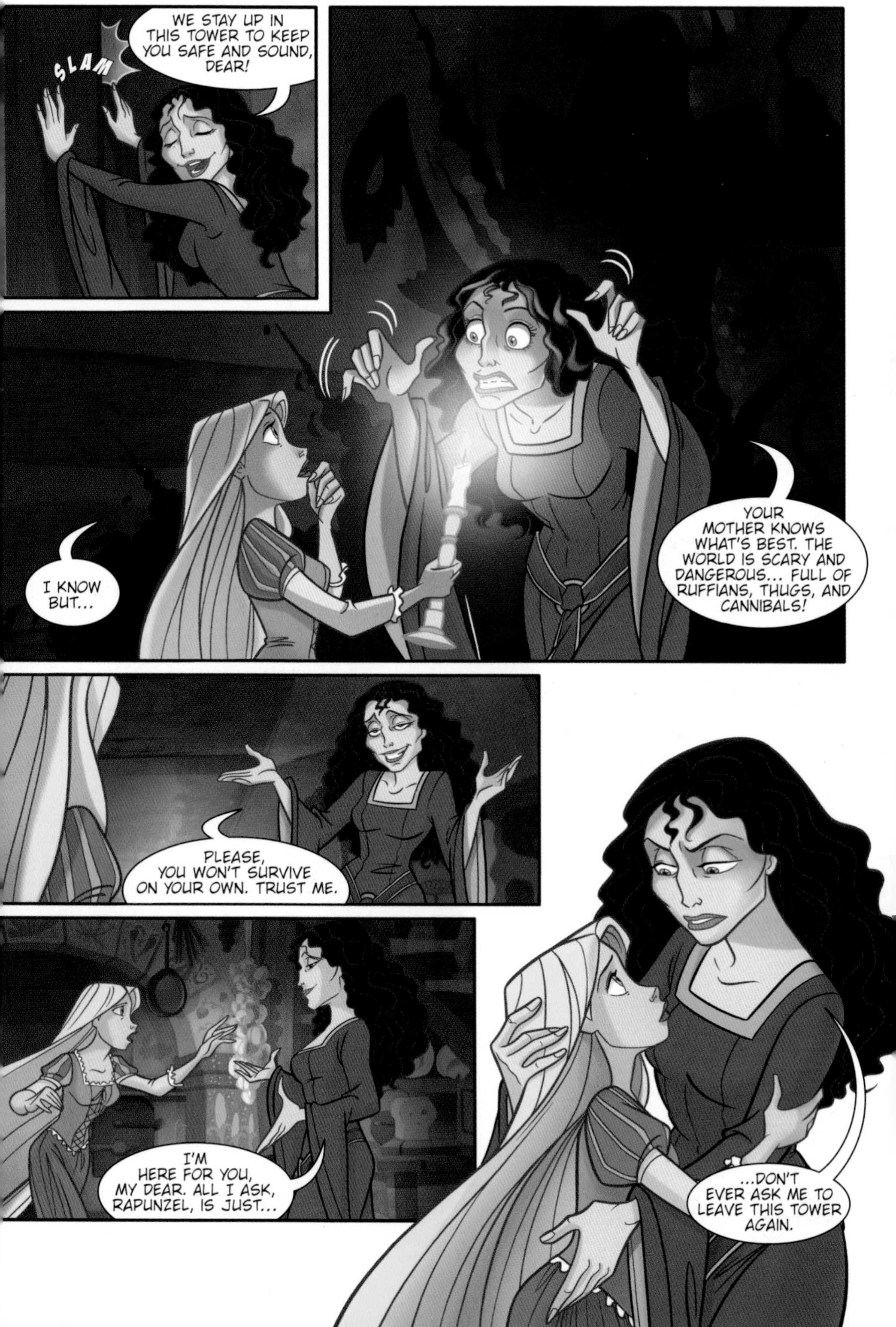
SLAM
WE STAY UP IN THIS TOWER TO KEEP YOU SAFE AND SOUND, DEAR!
I KNOW BUT...
YOUR MOTHER KNOWS WHAT'S BEST. THE WORLD IS SCARY AND DANGEROUS... FULL OF RUFFIANS, THUGS, AND CANNIBALS!
PLEASE, YOU WON'T SURVIVE ON YOUR OWN. TRUST ME.
I'M HERE FOR YOU, MY DEAR. ALL I ASK, RAPUNZEL, IS JUST...
...DON'T EVER ASK ME TO LEAVE THIS TOWER AGAIN.

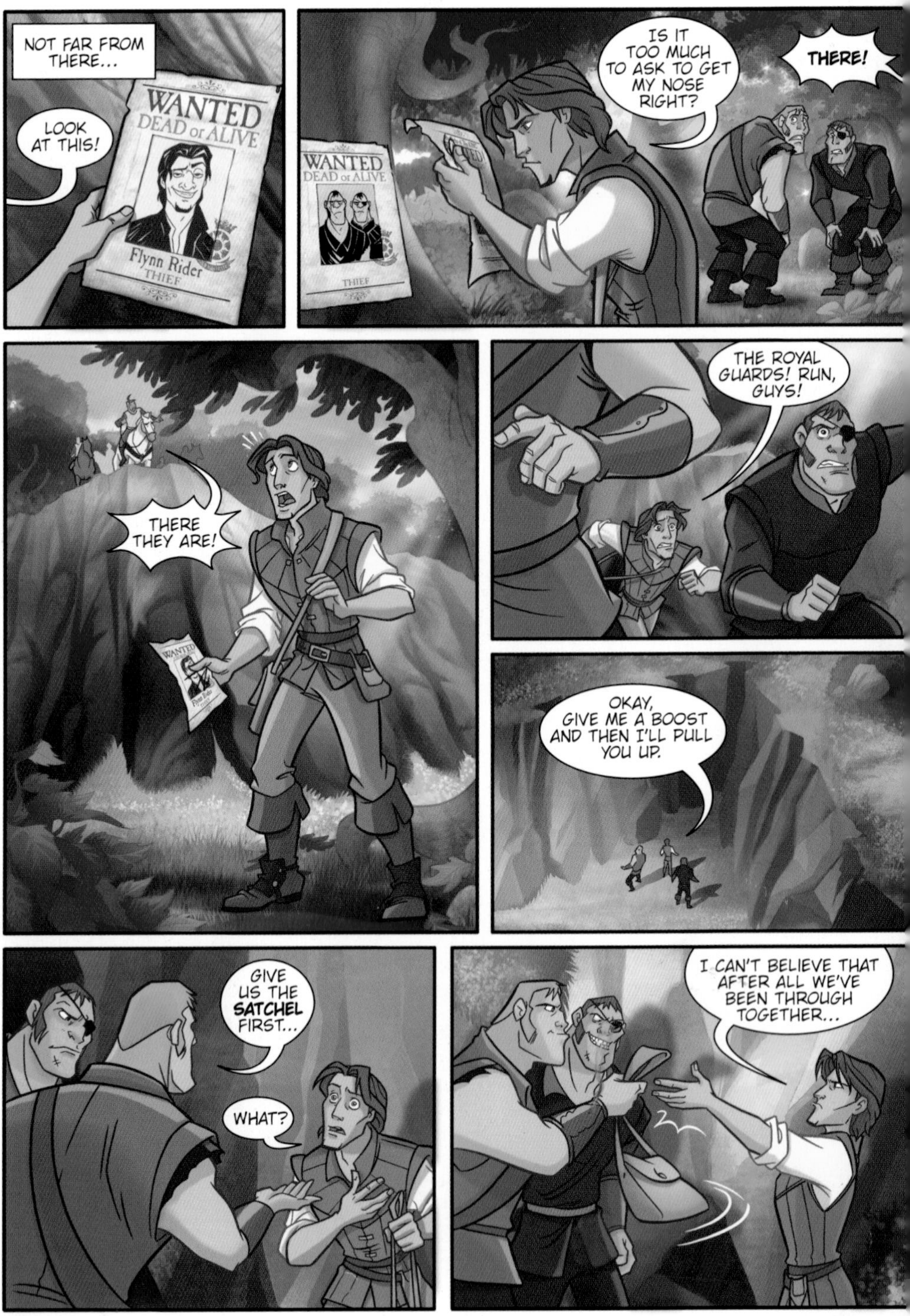
NOT FAR FROM THERE...
LOOK AT THIS!
WANTED
DEAD or ALIVE
Flynn Rider
THIEF
WANTED
DEAD or ALIVE
THIEF
IS IT TOO MUCH TO ASK TO GET MY NOSE RIGHT?
THERE!
THERE THEY ARE!
THE ROYAL GUARDS! RUN, GUYS!
OKAY, GIVE ME A BOOST AND THEN I'LL PULL YOU UP.
GIVE US THE SATCHEL FIRST...
WHAT?
I CAN'T BELIEVE THAT AFTER ALL WE'VE BEEN THROUGH TOGETHER...

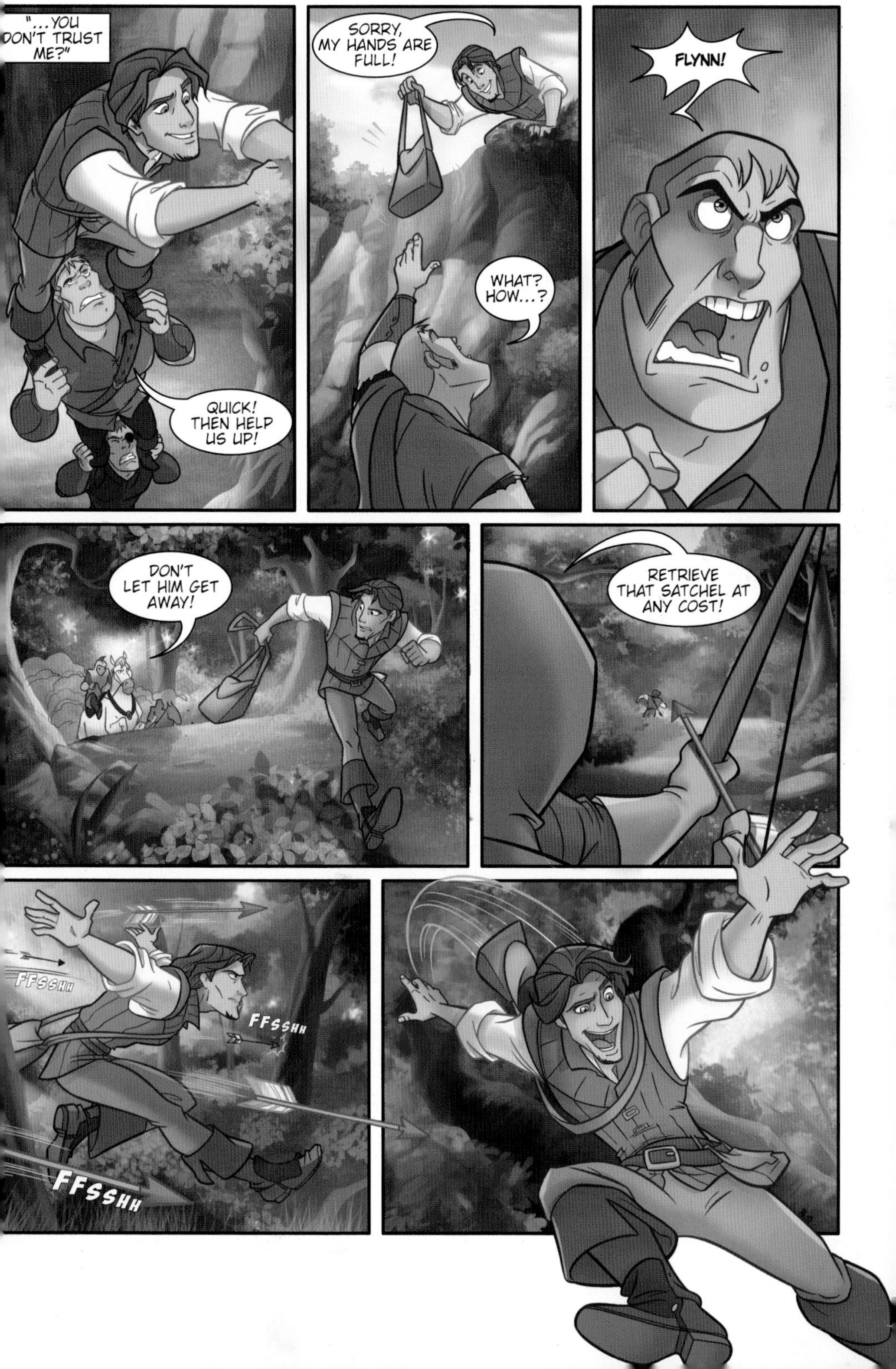
"...YOU
DON'T TRUST
ME?"
QUICK!
THEN HELP
US UP!
SORRY,
MY HANDS ARE
FULL!
WHAT?
HOW...?
FLYNN!
DON'T
LET HIM GET
AWAY!
RETRIEVE
THAT SATCHEL AT
ANY COST!
FFSSHH
FFSSHH
FFSSHH

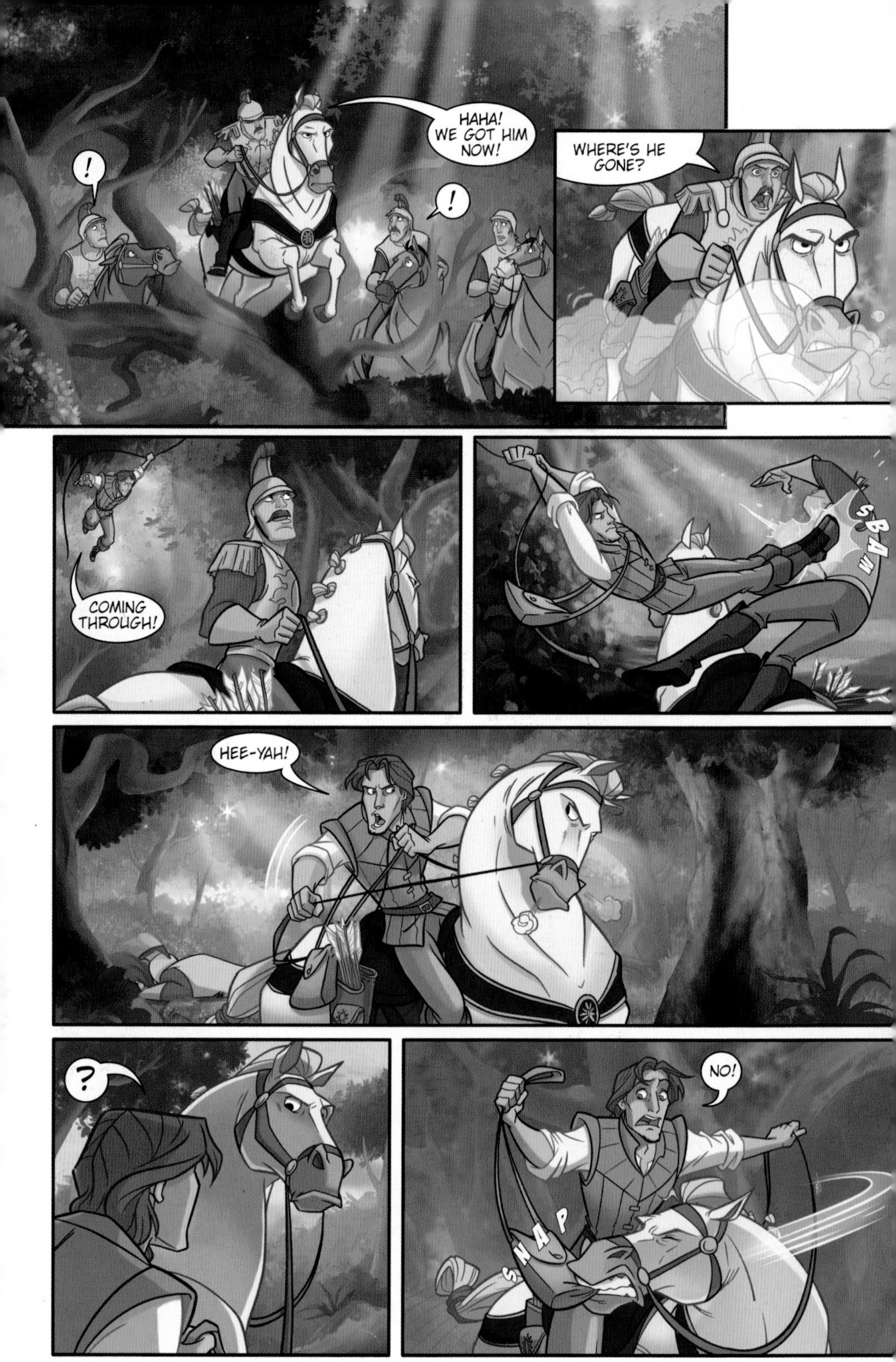

!
HAHA! WE GOT HIM NOW!
!
WHERE'S HE GONE?
COMING THROUGH!
SBAM
HEE-YAH!
?
NO!
SNAP

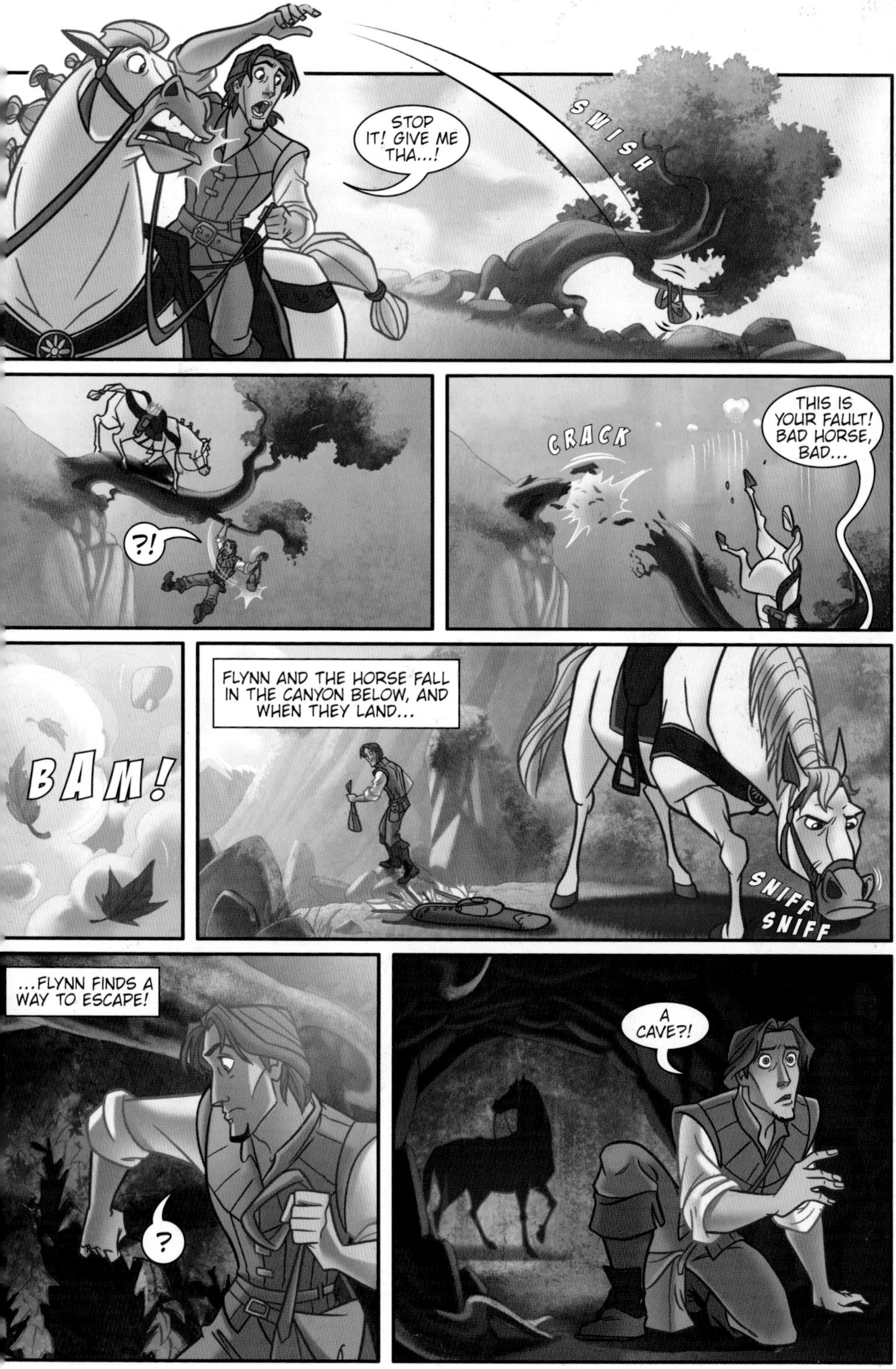
STOP IT! GIVE ME THA...!
SWISH
?!
CRACK
THIS IS YOUR FAULT! BAD HORSE, BAD...
BAM!
FLYNN AND THE HORSE FALL IN THE CANYON BELOW, AND WHEN THEY LAND...
SNIFF SNIFF
...FLYNN FINDS A WAY TO ESCAPE!
?
A CAVE?!

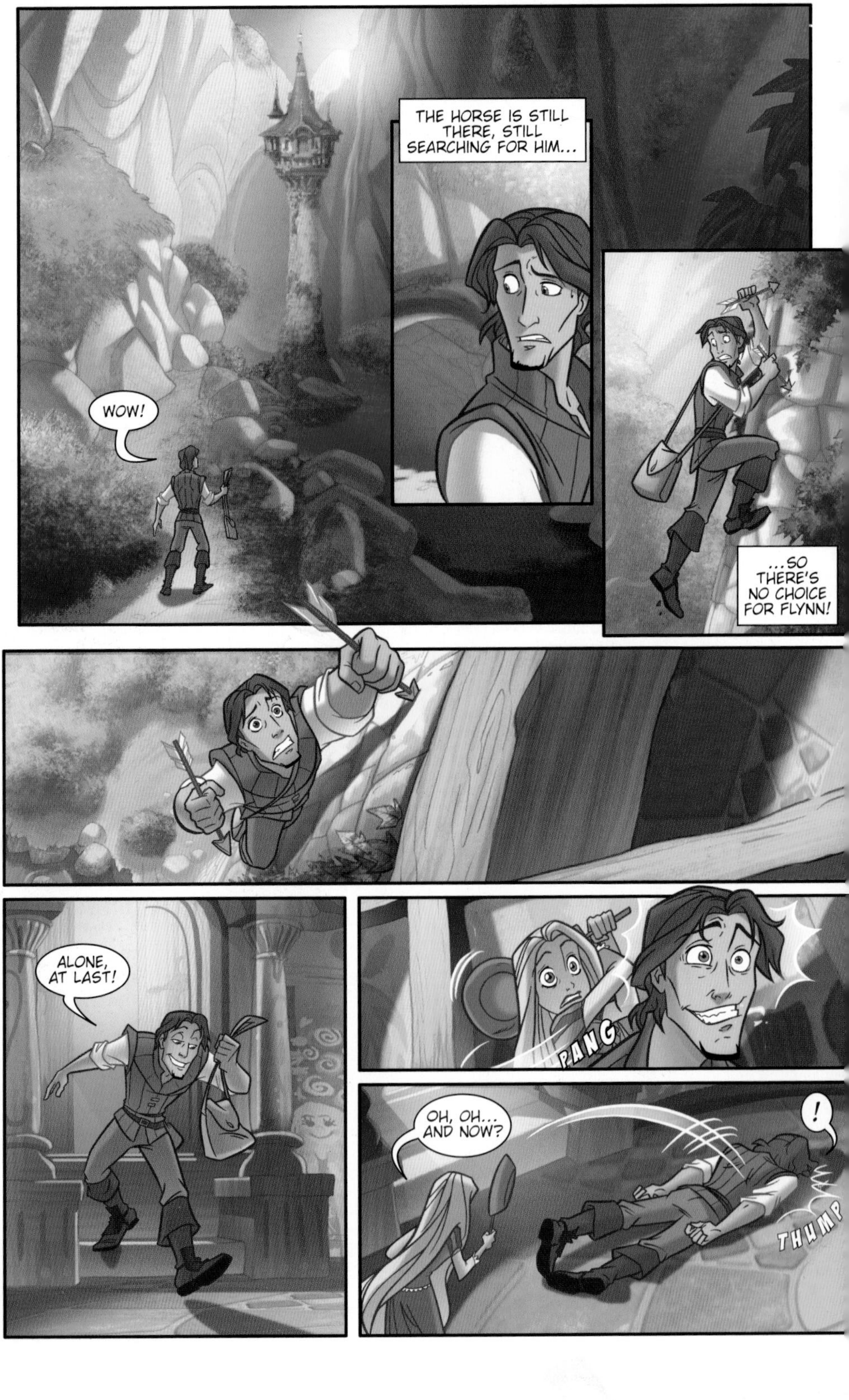
WOW!
THE HORSE IS STILL THERE, STILL SEARCHING FOR HIM...
...SO THERE'S NO CHOICE FOR FLYNN!
ALONE, AT LAST!
PANG
OH, OH... AND NOW?
!
THUMP

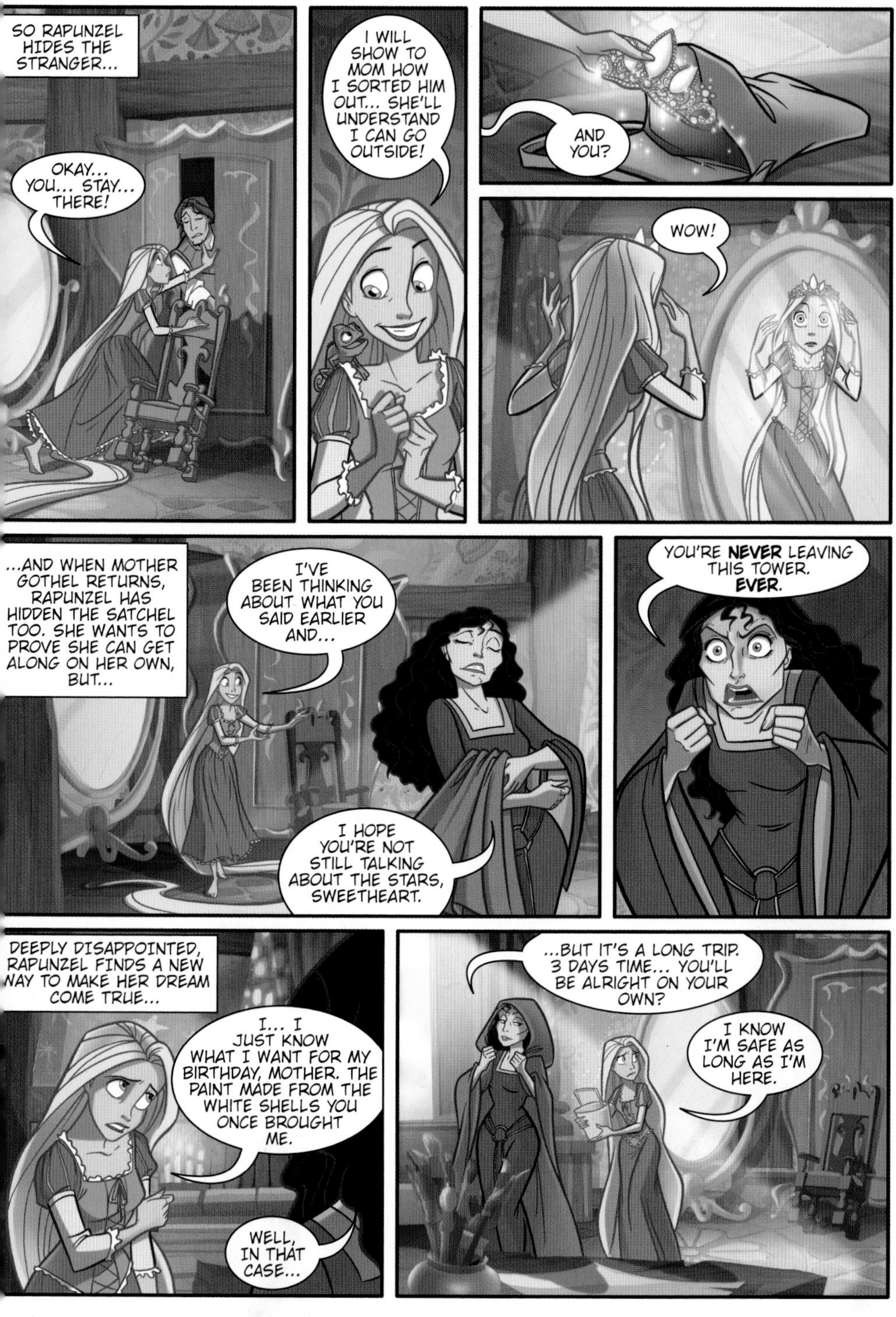
SO RAPUNZEL HIDES THE STRANGER...
OKAY... YOU... STAY... THERE!
I WILL SHOW TO MOM HOW I SORTED HIM OUT... SHE'LL UNDERSTAND I CAN GO OUTSIDE!
AND YOU?
WOW!
...AND WHEN MOTHER GOTHEL RETURNS, RAPUNZEL HAS HIDDEN THE SATCHEL TOO. SHE WANTS TO PROVE SHE CAN GET ALONG ON HER OWN, BUT...
I'VE BEEN THINKING ABOUT WHAT YOU SAID EARLIER AND...
I HOPE YOU'RE NOT STILL TALKING ABOUT THE STARS, SWEETHEART.
YOU'RE **NEVER** LEAVING THIS TOWER. **EVER**.
DEEPLY DISAPPOINTED, RAPUNZEL FINDS A NEW WAY TO MAKE HER DREAM COME TRUE...
I... I JUST KNOW WHAT I WANT FOR MY BIRTHDAY, MOTHER. THE PAINT MADE FROM THE WHITE SHELLS YOU ONCE BROUGHT ME.
WELL, IN THAT CASE...
...BUT IT'S A LONG TRIP. 3 DAYS TIME... YOU'LL BE ALRIGHT ON YOUR OWN?
I KNOW I'M SAFE AS LONG AS I'M HERE.

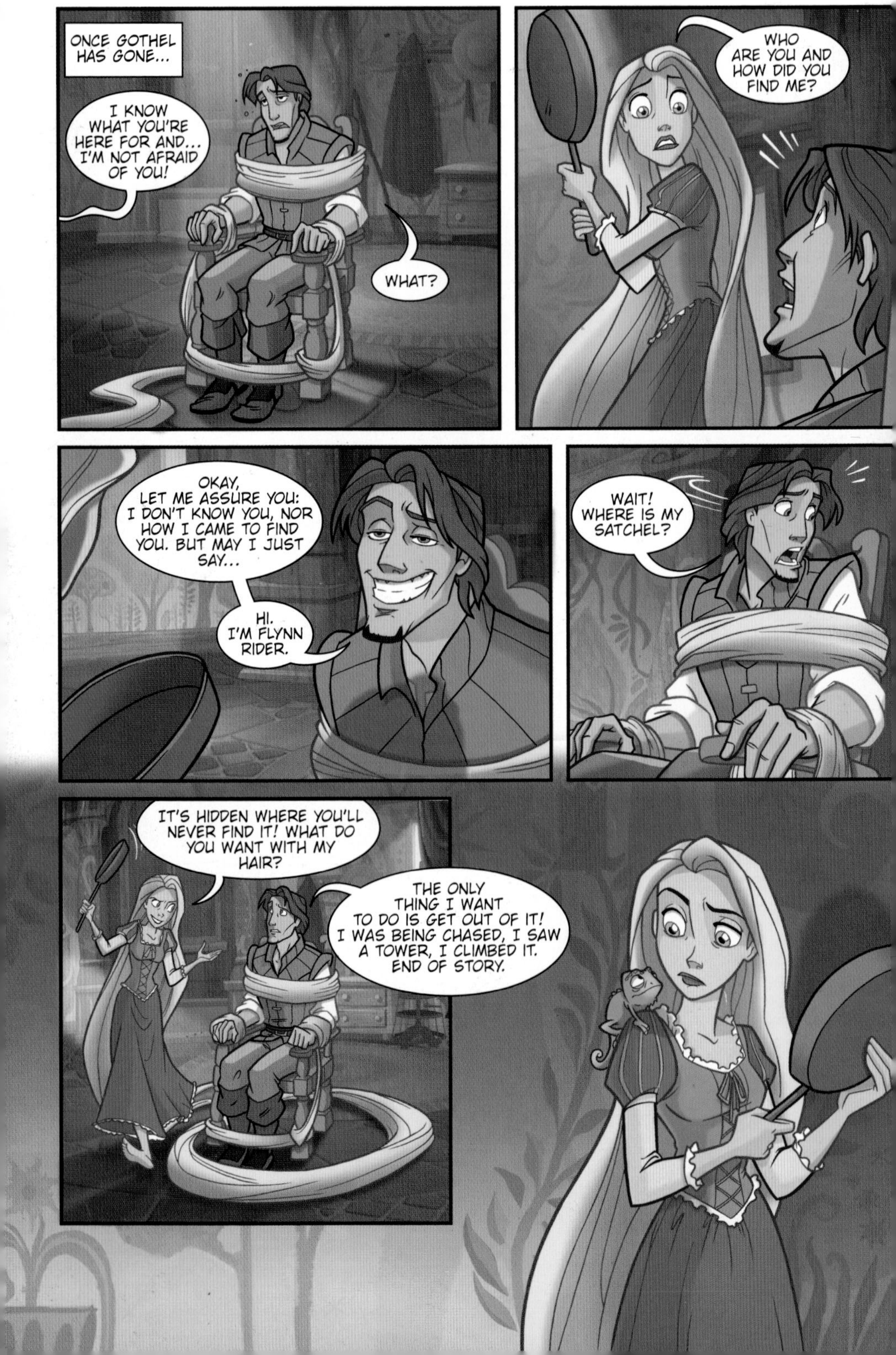
ONCE GOTHEL HAS GONE...
I KNOW WHAT YOU'RE HERE FOR AND... I'M NOT AFRAID OF YOU!
WHAT?
WHO ARE YOU AND HOW DID YOU FIND ME?
OKAY, LET ME ASSURE YOU: I DON'T KNOW YOU, NOR HOW I CAME TO FIND YOU. BUT MAY I JUST SAY...
HI. I'M FLYNN RIDER.
WAIT! WHERE IS MY SATCHEL?
IT'S HIDDEN WHERE YOU'LL NEVER FIND IT! WHAT DO YOU WANT WITH MY HAIR?
THE ONLY THING I WANT TO DO IS GET OUT OF IT! I WAS BEING CHASED, I SAW A TOWER, I CLIMBED IT. END OF STORY.

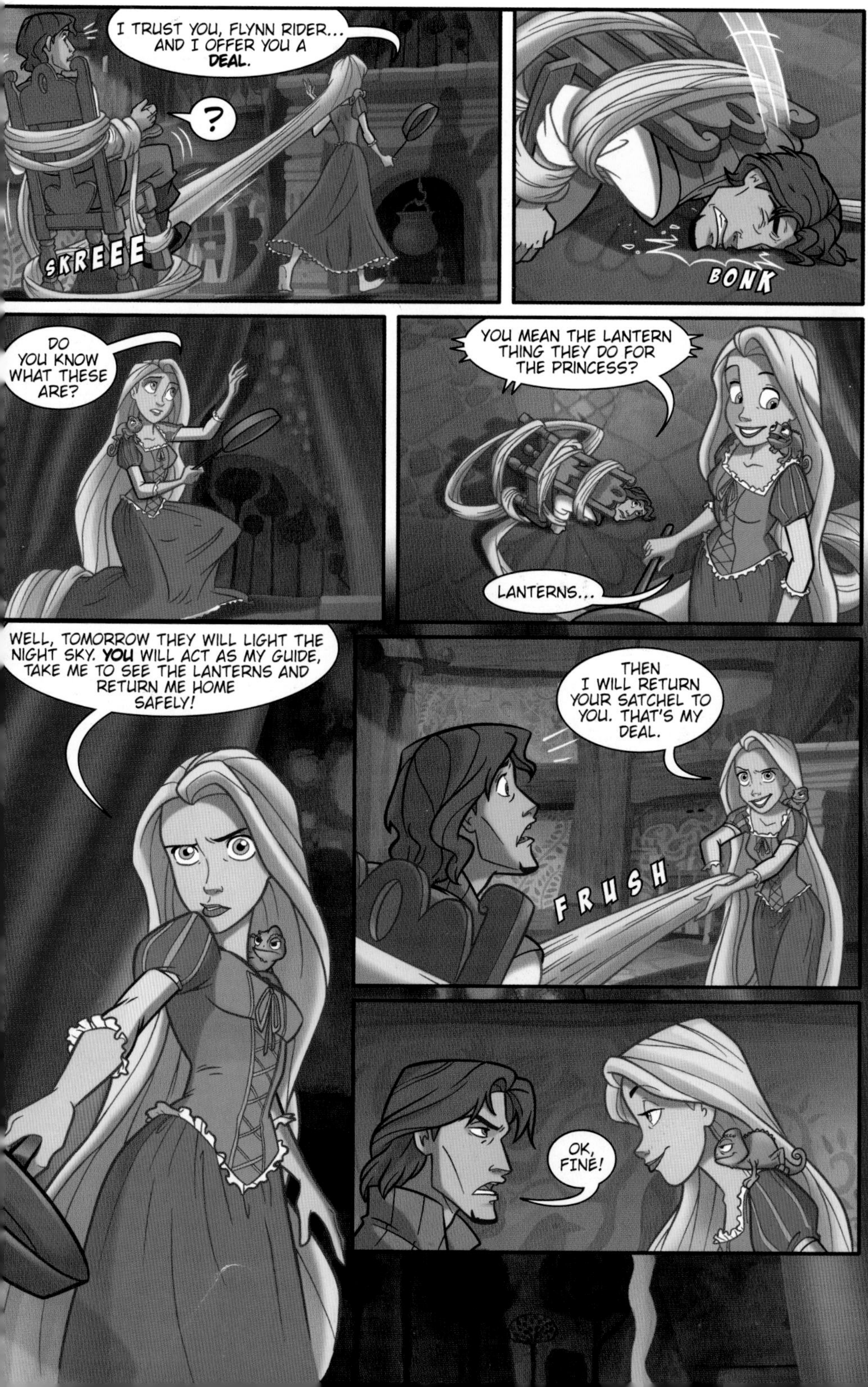
I TRUST YOU, FLYNN RIDER... AND I OFFER YOU A **DEAL**.
?
SKREEE
BONK
DO YOU KNOW WHAT THESE ARE?
YOU MEAN THE LANTERN THING THEY DO FOR THE PRINCESS?
LANTERNS...
WELL, TOMORROW THEY WILL LIGHT THE NIGHT SKY. **YOU** WILL ACT AS MY GUIDE, TAKE ME TO SEE THE LANTERNS AND RETURN ME HOME SAFELY!
THEN I WILL RETURN YOUR SATCHEL TO YOU. THAT'S MY DEAL.
FRUSH
OK, FINE!

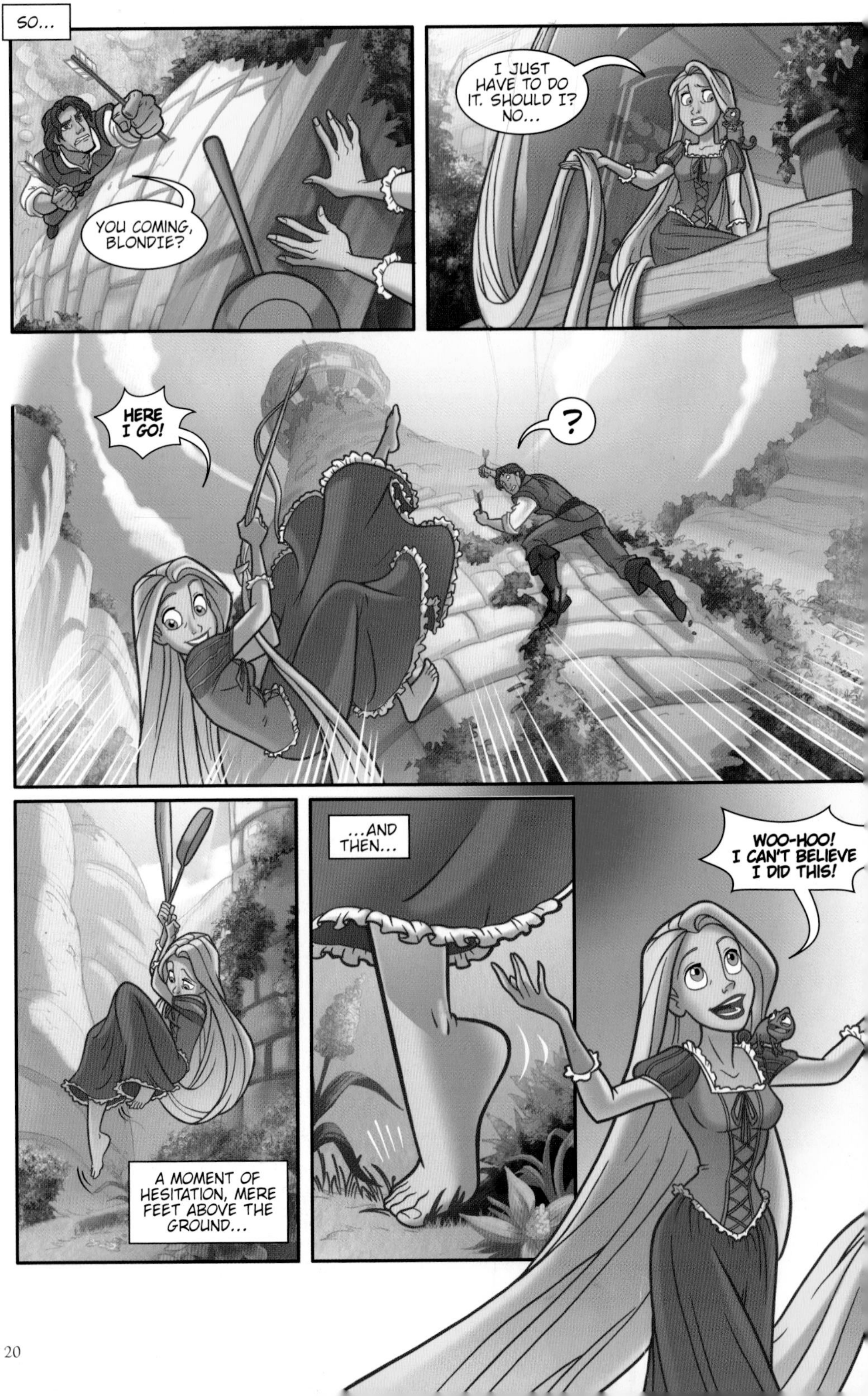
SO...
YOU COMING, BLONDIE?
I JUST HAVE TO DO IT. SHOULD I? NO...
HERE I GO!
?
A MOMENT OF HESITATION, MERE FEET ABOVE THE GROUND...
...AND THEN...
WOO-HOO! I CAN'T BELIEVE I DID THIS!

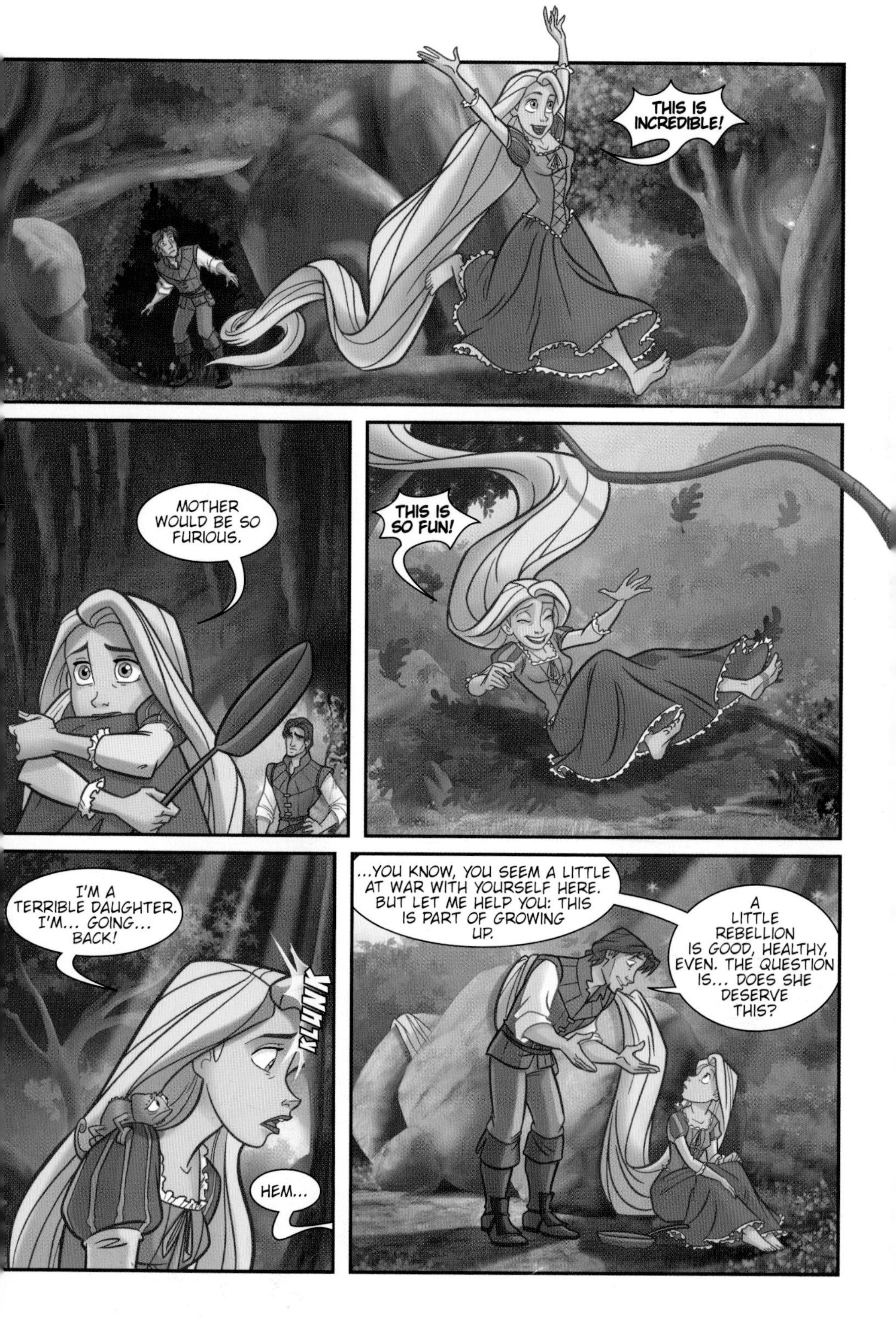
THIS IS INCREDIBLE!
MOTHER WOULD BE SO FURIOUS.
THIS IS SO FUN!
I'M A TERRIBLE DAUGHTER. I'M... GOING... BACK!
KLUNK
HEM...
...YOU KNOW, YOU SEEM A LITTLE AT WAR WITH YOURSELF HERE. BUT LET ME HELP YOU: THIS IS PART OF GROWING UP.
A LITTLE REBELLION IS GOOD, HEALTHY, EVEN. THE QUESTION IS... DOES SHE DESERVE THIS?

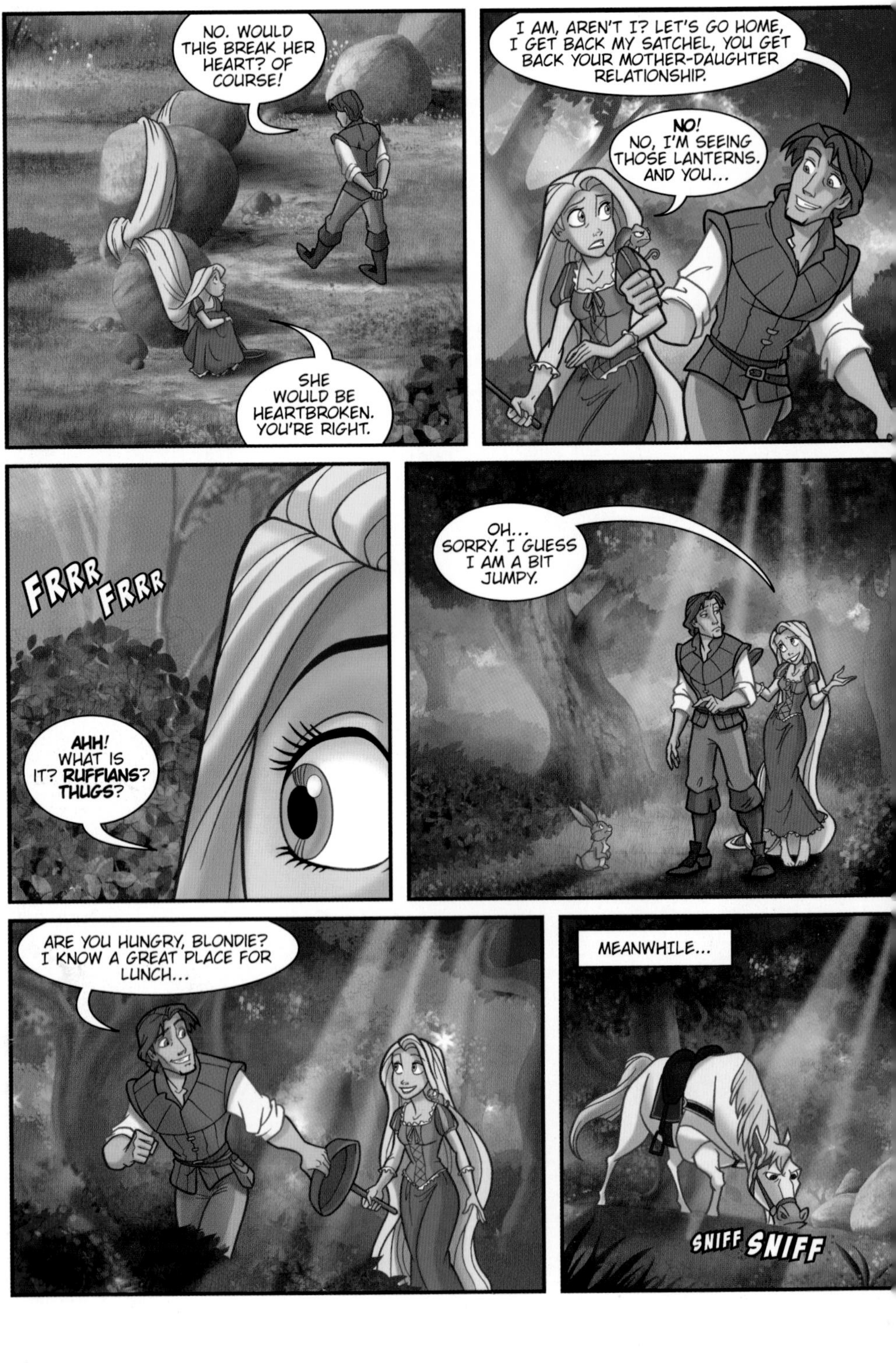
NO. WOULD THIS BREAK HER HEART? OF COURSE!
SHE WOULD BE HEARTBROKEN. YOU'RE RIGHT.
I AM, AREN'T I? LET'S GO HOME, I GET BACK MY SATCHEL, YOU GET BACK YOUR MOTHER-DAUGHTER RELATIONSHIP.
NO! NO, I'M SEEING THOSE LANTERNS. AND YOU...
FRRR FRRR
AHH! WHAT IS IT? RUFFIANS? THUGS?
OH... SORRY. I GUESS I AM A BIT JUMPY.
ARE YOU HUNGRY, BLONDIE? I KNOW A GREAT PLACE FOR LUNCH...
MEANWHILE...
SNIFF SNIFF

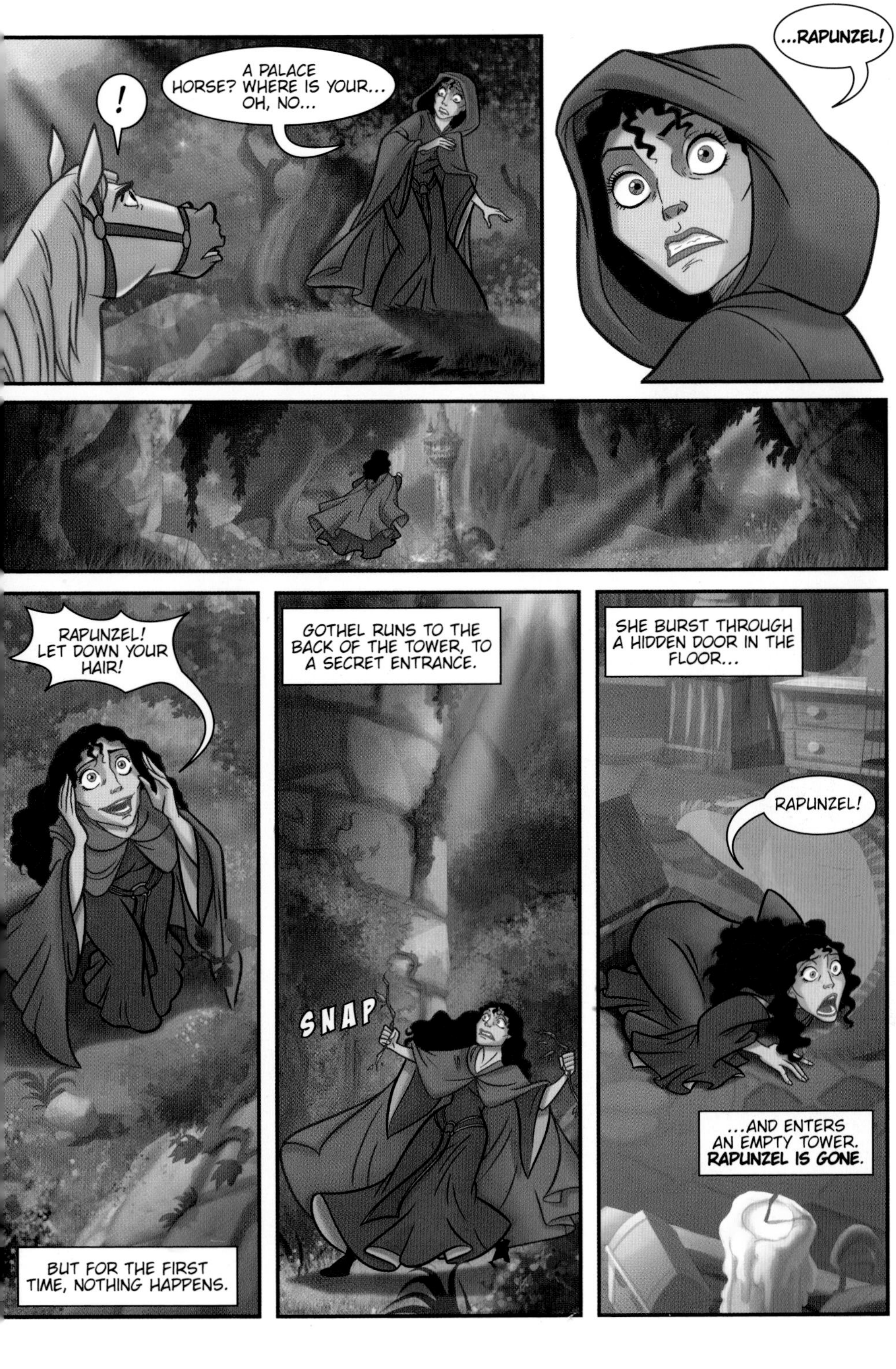
!
A PALACE HORSE? WHERE IS YOUR... OH, NO...
...RAPUNZEL!
RAPUNZEL! LET DOWN YOUR HAIR!
BUT FOR THE FIRST TIME, NOTHING HAPPENS.
GOTHEL RUNS TO THE BACK OF THE TOWER, TO A SECRET ENTRANCE.
SNAP
SHE BURST THROUGH A HIDDEN DOOR IN THE FLOOR...
RAPUNZEL!
...AND ENTERS AN EMPTY TOWER. RAPUNZEL IS GONE.

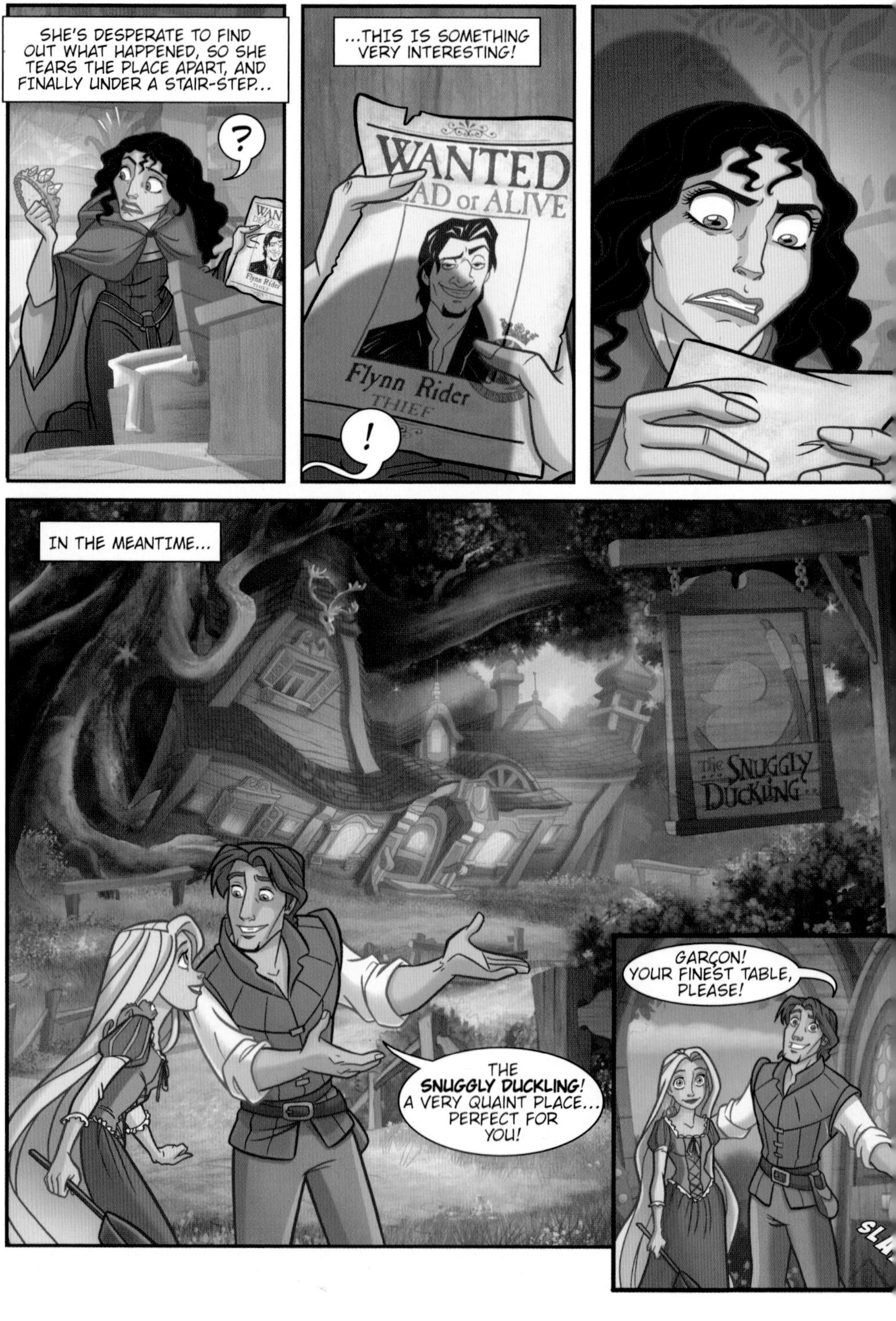
SHE'S DESPERATE TO FIND OUT WHAT HAPPENED, SO SHE TEARS THE PLACE APART, AND FINALLY UNDER A STAIR-STEP...
?
...THIS IS SOMETHING VERY INTERESTING!
WANTED
EAD or ALIVE
Flynn Rider
THIEF
!
IN THE MEANTIME...
The SNUGGLY DUCKLING
THE SNUGGLY DUCKLING! A VERY QUAINT PLACE... PERFECT FOR YOU!
GARÇON! YOUR FINEST TABLE, PLEASE!

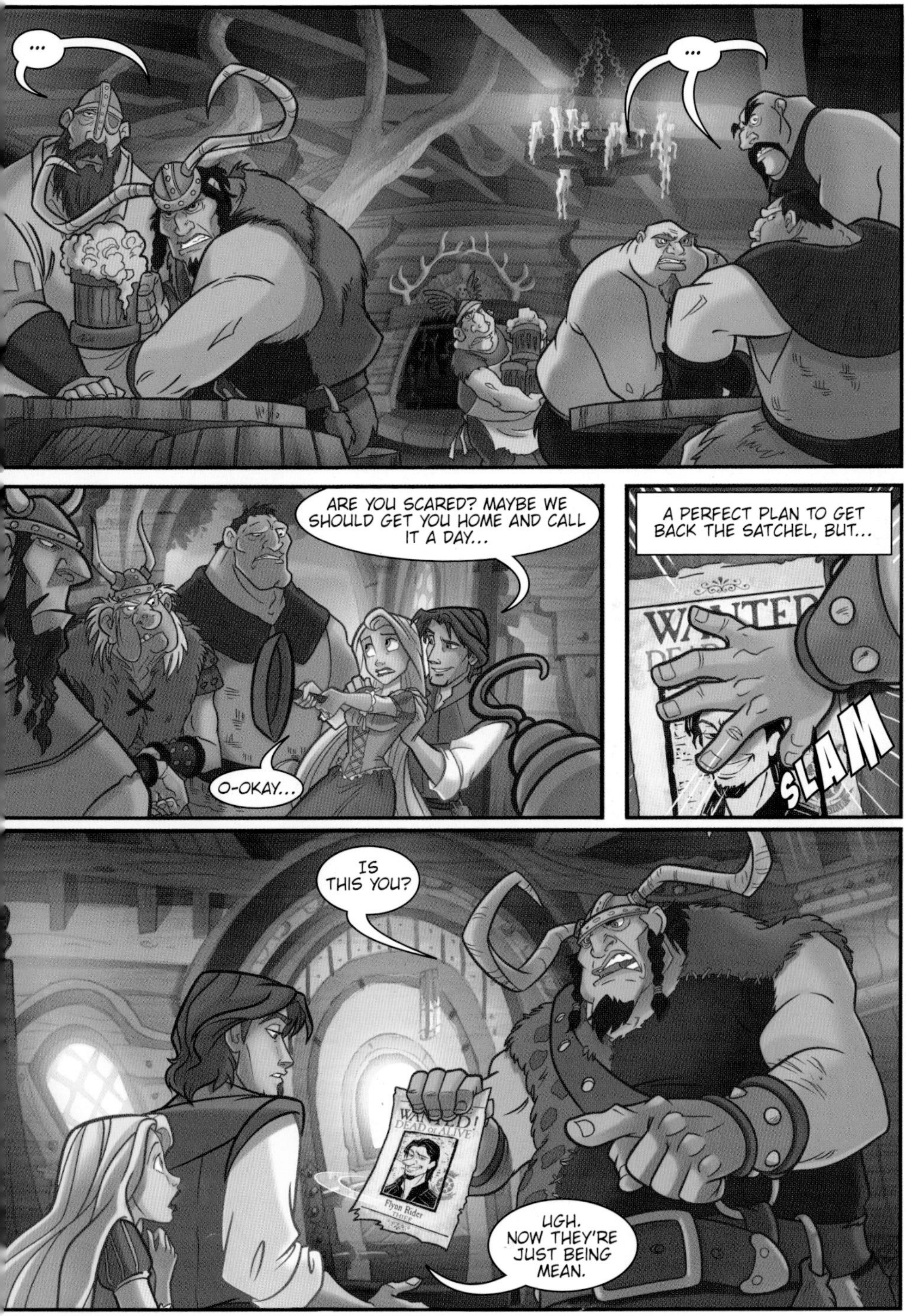
...
...
ARE YOU SCARED? MAYBE WE SHOULD GET YOU HOME AND CALL IT A DAY...
O-OKAY...
A PERFECT PLAN TO GET BACK THE SATCHEL, BUT...
SLAM
IS THIS YOU?
WANTED! DEAD or ALIVE
Flynn Rider
UGH. NOW THEY'RE JUST BEING MEAN.

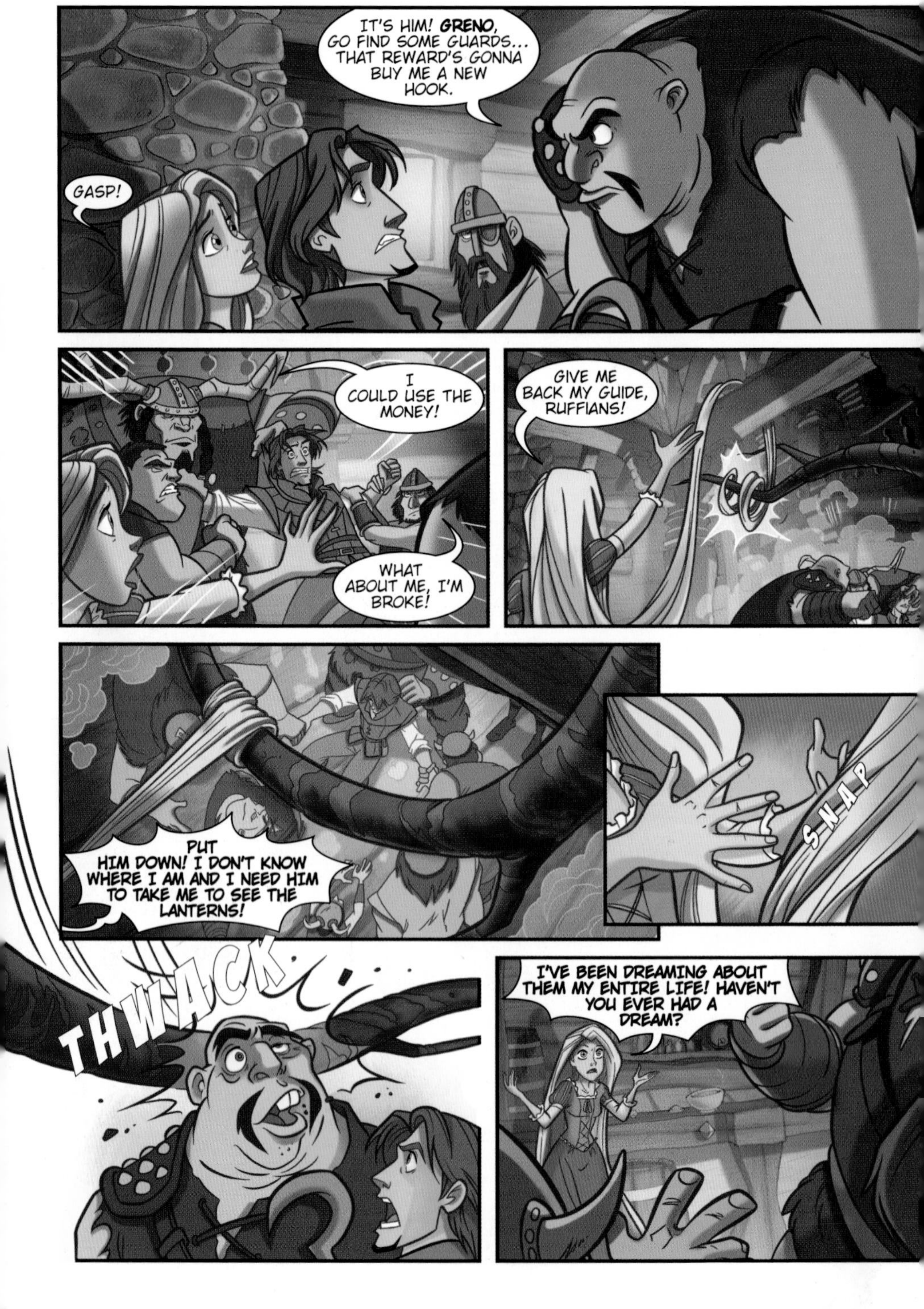
IT'S HIM! GRENO, GO FIND SOME GUARDS... THAT REWARD'S GONNA BUY ME A NEW HOOK.
GASP!
I COULD USE THE MONEY!
WHAT ABOUT ME, I'M BROKE!
GIVE ME BACK MY GUIDE, RUFFIANS!
PUT HIM DOWN! I DON'T KNOW WHERE I AM AND I NEED HIM TO TAKE ME TO SEE THE LANTERNS!
SNAP
THWACK
I'VE BEEN DREAMING ABOUT THEM MY ENTIRE LIFE! HAVEN'T YOU EVER HAD A DREAM?

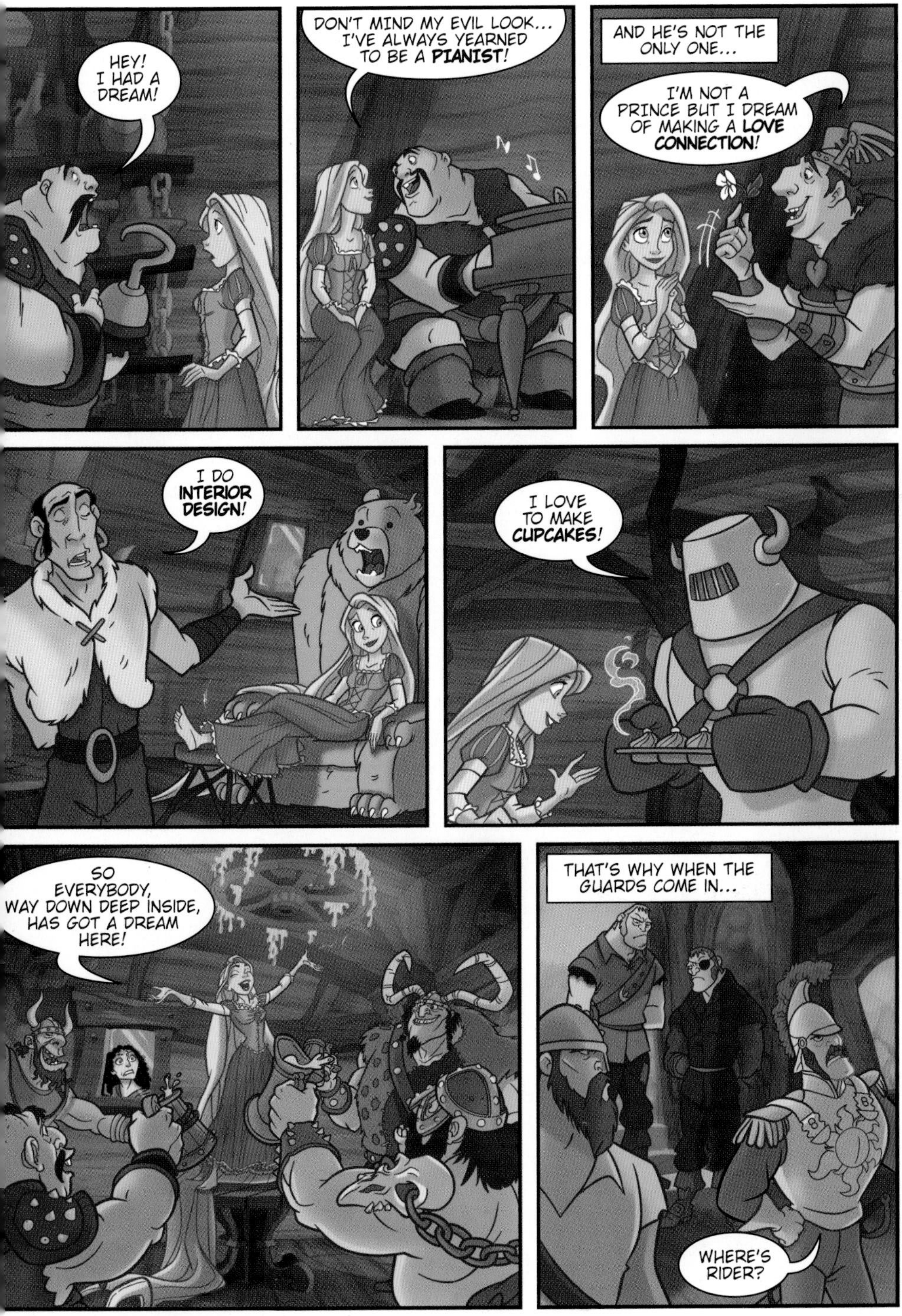
HEY! I HAD A DREAM!
DON'T MIND MY EVIL LOOK... I'VE ALWAYS YEARNED TO BE A **PIANIST**!
AND HE'S NOT THE ONLY ONE...
I'M NOT A PRINCE BUT I DREAM OF MAKING A **LOVE CONNECTION**!
I DO **INTERIOR DESIGN**!
I LOVE TO MAKE **CUPCAKES**!
SO EVERYBODY, WAY DOWN DEEP INSIDE, HAS GOT A DREAM HERE!
THAT'S WHY WHEN THE GUARDS COME IN...
WHERE'S RIDER?

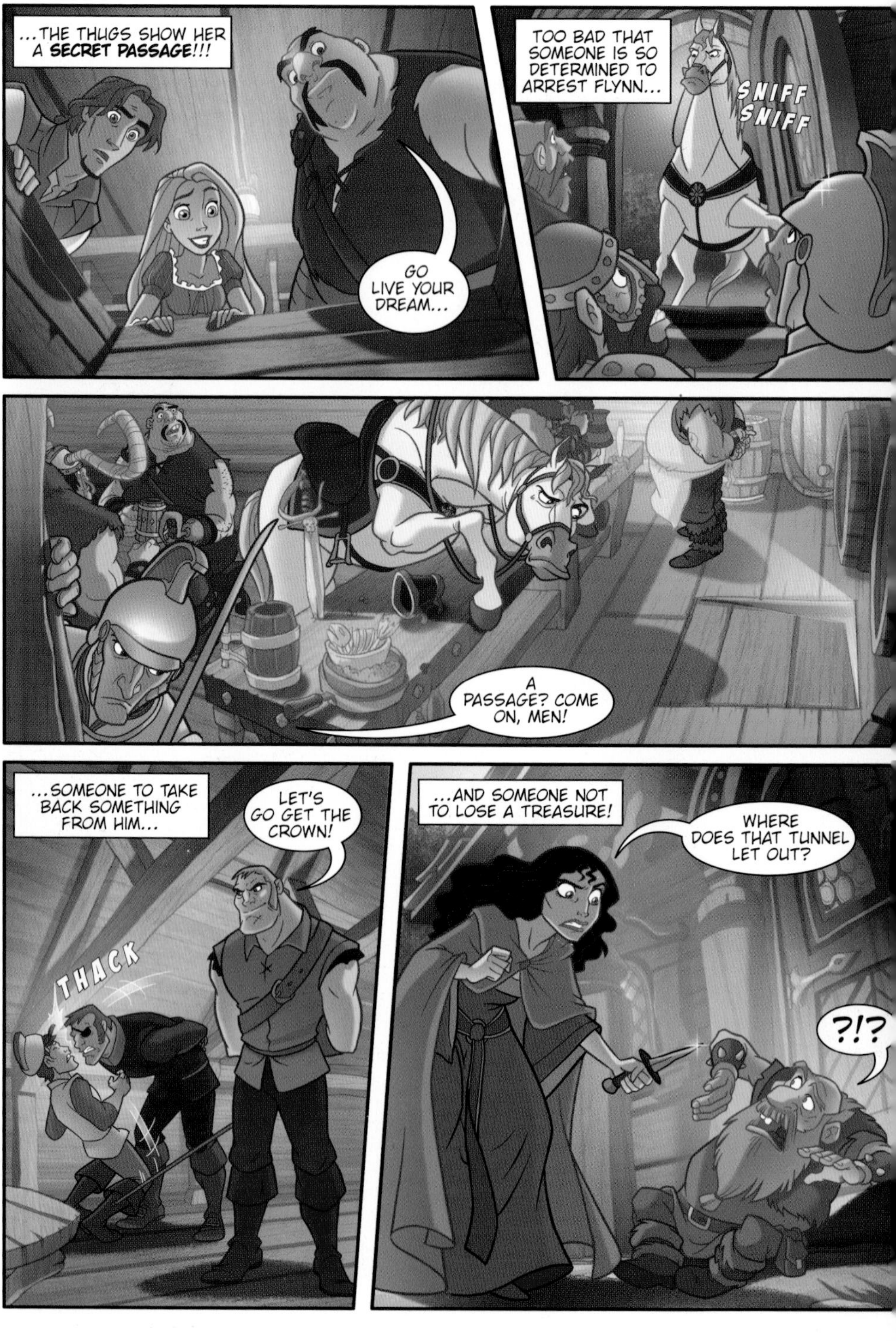
...THE THUGS SHOW HER A SECRET PASSAGE!!!
GO LIVE YOUR DREAM...
TOO BAD THAT SOMEONE IS SO DETERMINED TO ARREST FLYNN...
SNIFF SNIFF
A PASSAGE? COME ON, MEN!
...SOMEONE TO TAKE BACK SOMETHING FROM HIM...
LET'S GO GET THE CROWN!
THACK
...AND SOMEONE NOT TO LOSE A TREASURE!
WHERE DOES THAT TUNNEL LET OUT?
?!?

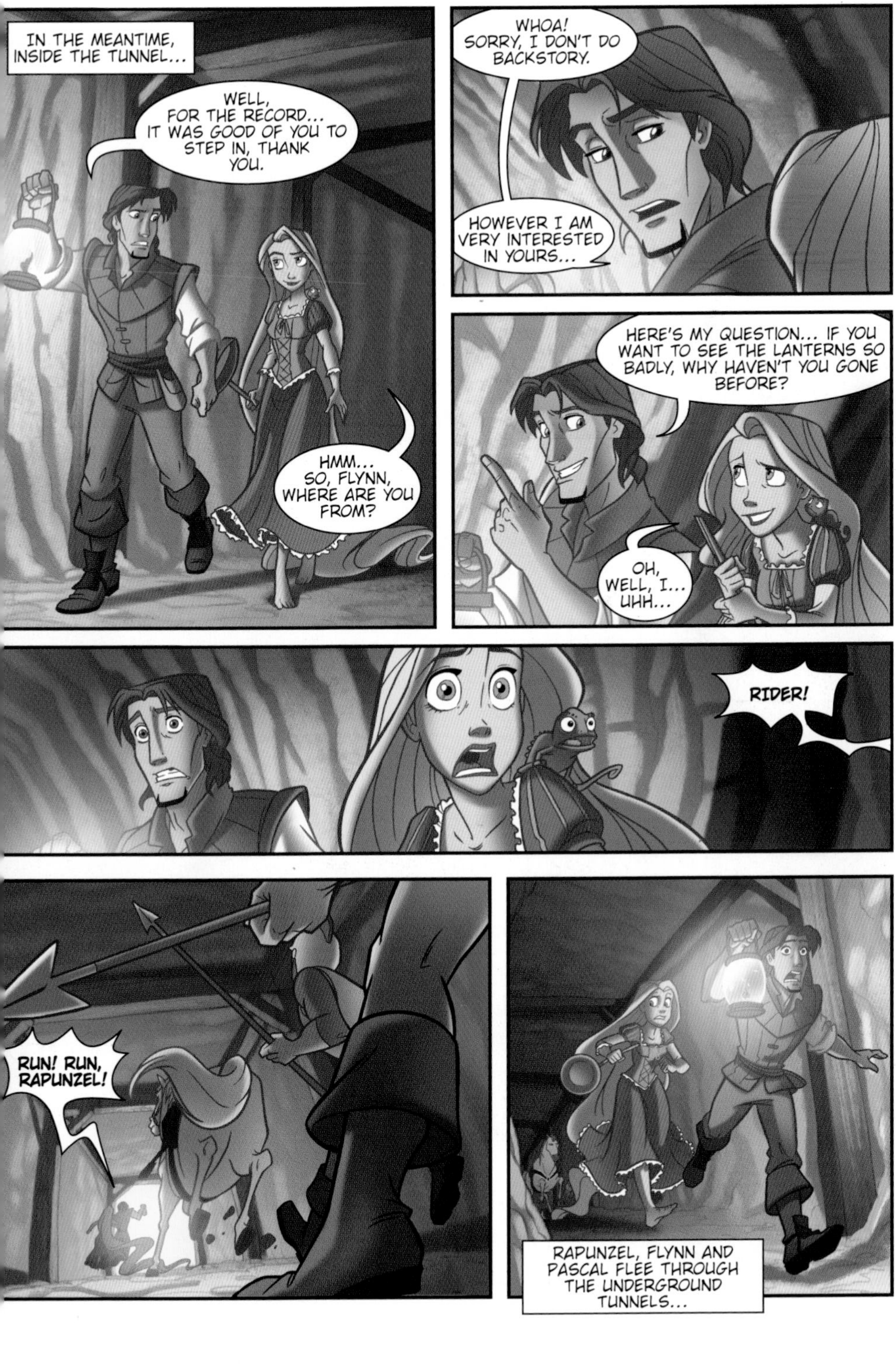
IN THE MEANTIME, INSIDE THE TUNNEL...
WELL, FOR THE RECORD... IT WAS GOOD OF YOU TO STEP IN, THANK YOU.
HMM... SO, FLYNN, WHERE ARE YOU FROM?
WHOA! SORRY, I DON'T DO BACKSTORY.
HOWEVER I AM VERY INTERESTED IN YOURS...
HERE'S MY QUESTION... IF YOU WANT TO SEE THE LANTERNS SO BADLY, WHY HAVEN'T YOU GONE BEFORE?
OH, WELL, I... UHH...
RIDER!
RUN! RUN, RAPUNZEL!
RAPUNZEL, FLYNN AND PASCAL FLEE THROUGH THE UNDERGROUND TUNNELS...

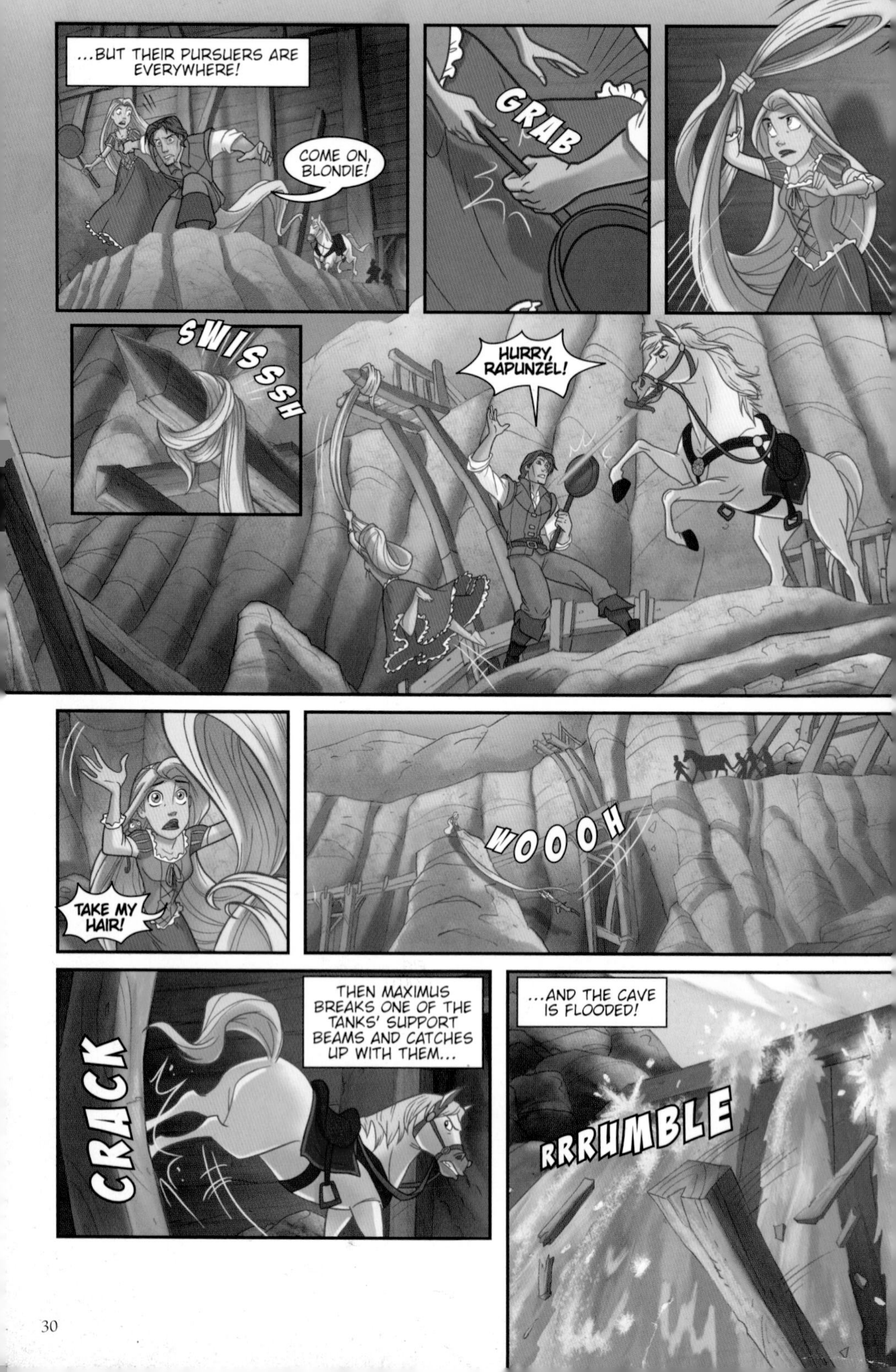

...BUT THEIR PURSUERS ARE EVERYWHERE!
COME ON, BLONDIE!
GRAB
SWISSSH
HURRY, RAPUNZEL!
TAKE MY HAIR!
WOOOH
THEN MAXIMUS BREAKS ONE OF THE TANKS' SUPPORT BEAMS AND CATCHES UP WITH THEM...
CRACK
...AND THE CAVE IS FLOODED!
RRRUMBLE

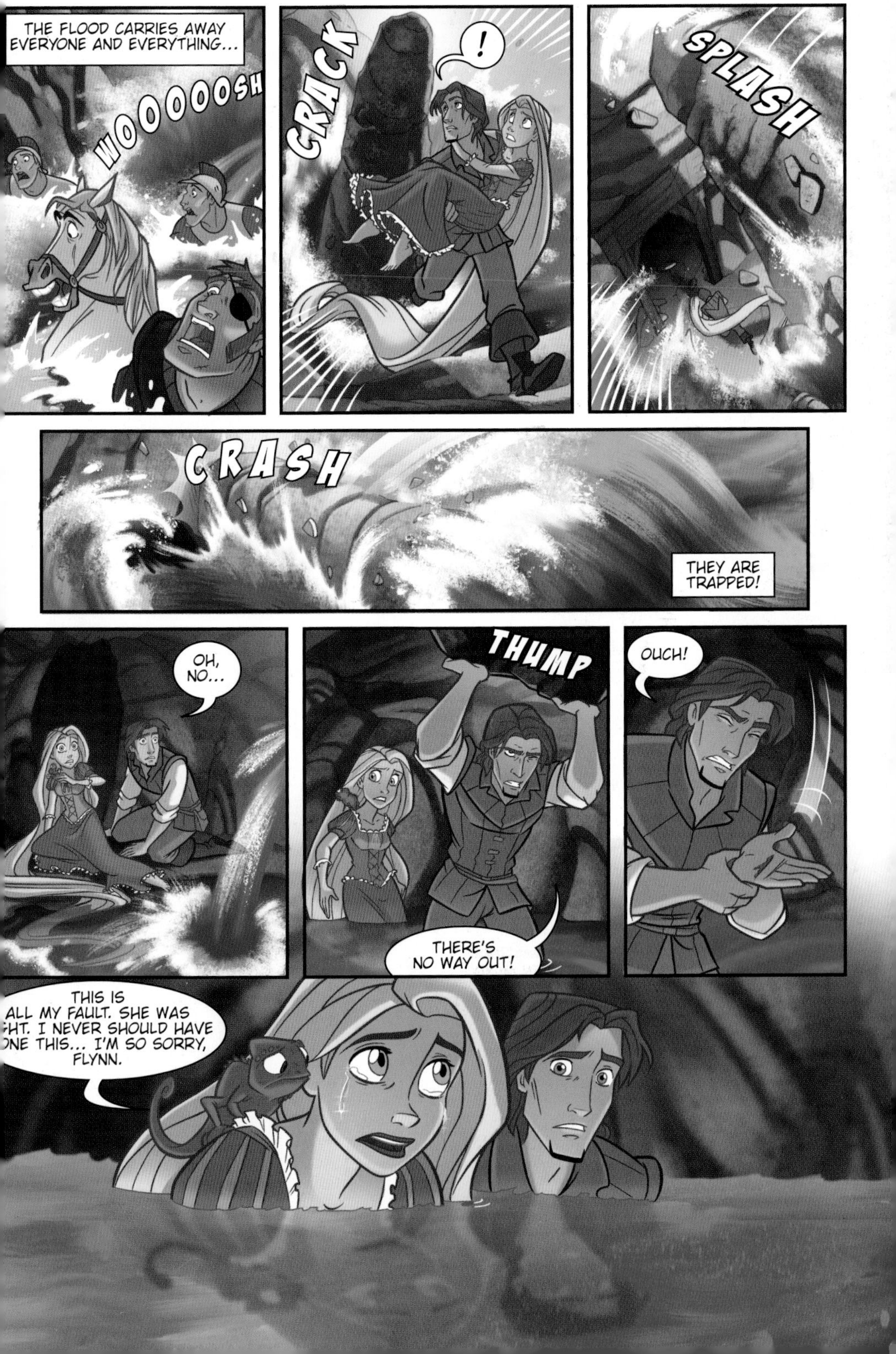
THE FLOOD CARRIES AWAY EVERYONE AND EVERYTHING...
WOOOOOOSH
CRACK
!
SPLASH
CRASH
THEY ARE TRAPPED!
OH, NO...
THUMP
THERE'S NO WAY OUT!
OUCH!
THIS IS
ALL MY FAULT. SHE WAS
GHT. I NEVER SHOULD HAVE
ONE THIS... I'M SO SORRY,
FLYNN.

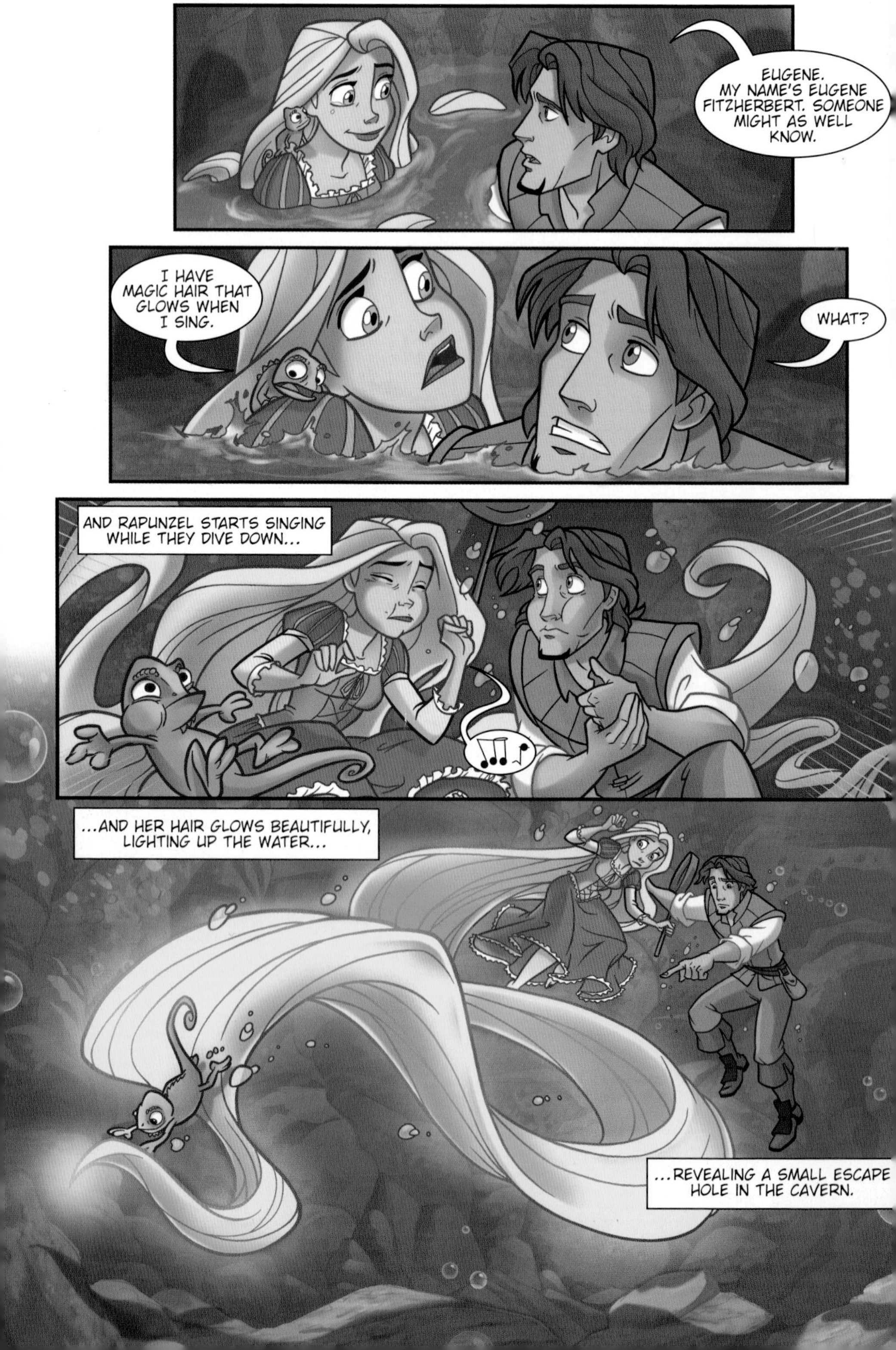
EUGENE.
MY NAME'S EUGENE FITZHERBERT. SOMEONE MIGHT AS WELL KNOW.
I HAVE MAGIC HAIR THAT GLOWS WHEN I SING.
WHAT?
AND RAPUNZEL STARTS SINGING WHILE THEY DIVE DOWN...
...AND HER HAIR GLOWS BEAUTIFULLY, LIGHTING UP THE WATER...
...REVEALING A SMALL ESCAPE HOLE IN THE CAVERN.

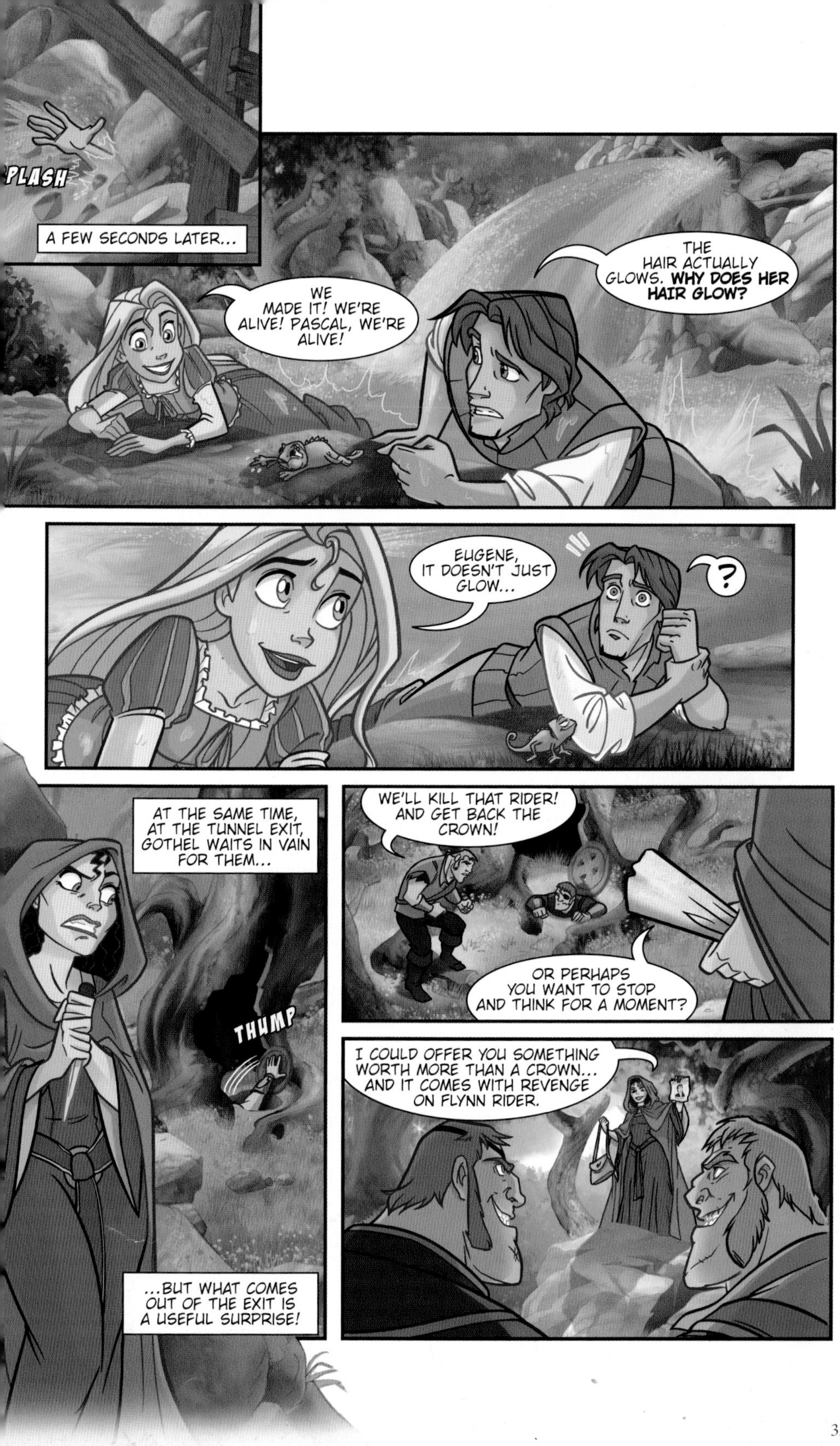

PLASH
A FEW SECONDS LATER...
WE MADE IT! WE'RE ALIVE! PASCAL, WE'RE ALIVE!
THE HAIR ACTUALLY GLOWS. WHY DOES HER HAIR GLOW?
EUGENE, IT DOESN'T JUST GLOW...
?
AT THE SAME TIME, AT THE TUNNEL EXIT, GOTHEL WAITS IN VAIN FOR THEM...
THUMP
...BUT WHAT COMES OUT OF THE EXIT IS A USEFUL SURPRISE!
WE'LL KILL THAT RIDER! AND GET BACK THE CROWN!
OR PERHAPS YOU WANT TO STOP AND THINK FOR A MOMENT?
I COULD OFFER YOU SOMETHING WORTH MORE THAN A CROWN... AND IT COMES WITH REVENGE ON FLYNN RIDER.

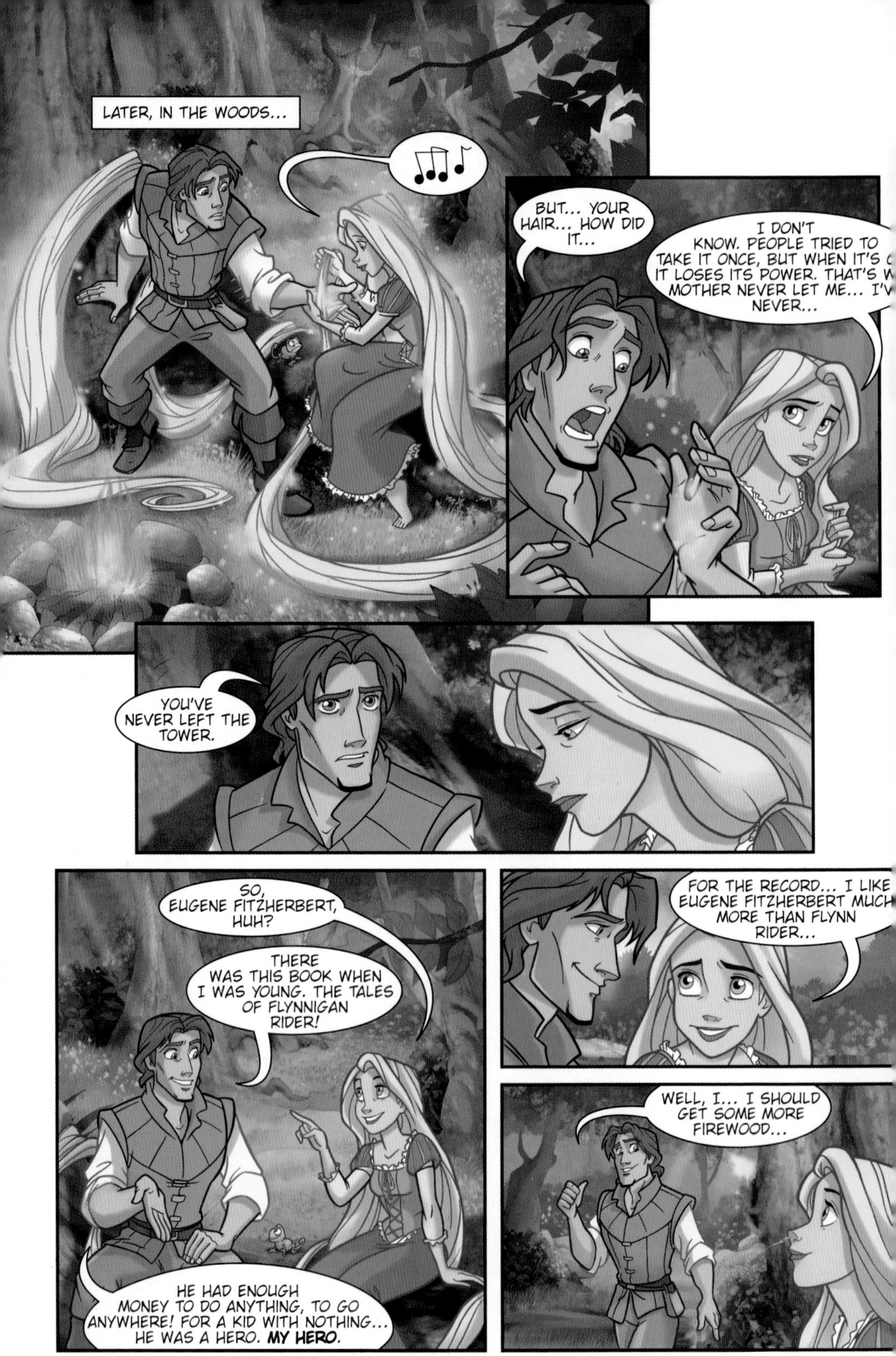
LATER, IN THE WOODS...
BUT... YOUR HAIR... HOW DID IT...
I DON'T KNOW. PEOPLE TRIED TO TAKE IT ONCE, BUT WHEN IT'S
IT LOSES ITS POWER. THAT'S
MOTHER NEVER LET ME... I'
NEVER...
YOU'VE NEVER LEFT THE TOWER.
SO, EUGENE FITZHERBERT, HUH?
THERE WAS THIS BOOK WHEN I WAS YOUNG. THE TALES OF FLYNNIGAN RIDER!
HE HAD ENOUGH MONEY TO DO ANYTHING, TO GO ANYWHERE! FOR A KID WITH NOTHING... HE WAS A HERO. MY HERO.
FOR THE RECORD... I LIKE EUGENE FITZHERBERT MUCH MORE THAN FLYNN RIDER...
WELL, I... I SHOULD GET SOME MORE FIREWOOD...

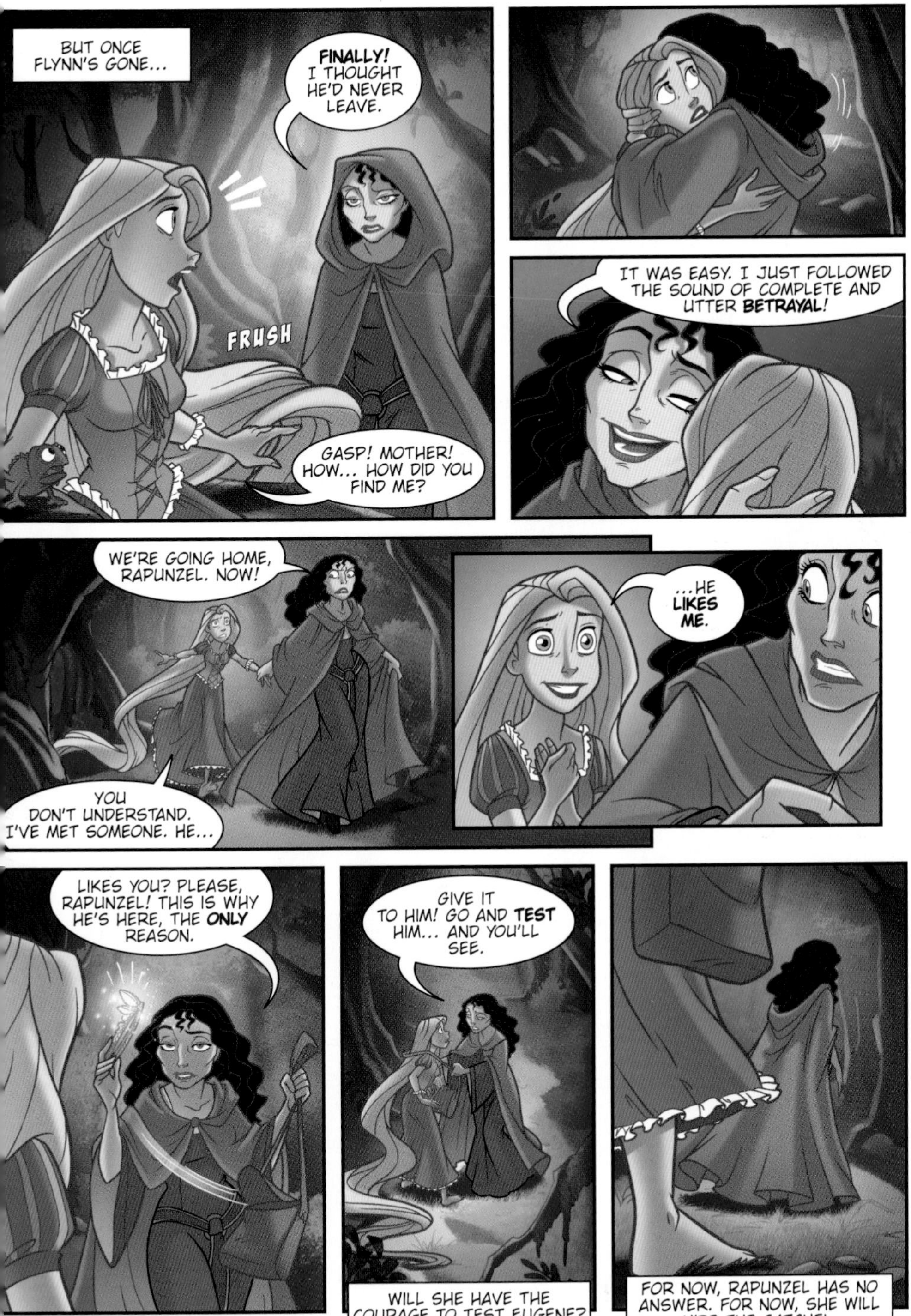

BUT ONCE FLYNN'S GONE...
FINALLY! I THOUGHT HE'D NEVER LEAVE.
FRUSH
GASP! MOTHER! HOW... HOW DID YOU FIND ME?
IT WAS EASY. I JUST FOLLOWED THE SOUND OF COMPLETE AND UTTER **BETRAYAL**!
WE'RE GOING HOME, RAPUNZEL. NOW!
YOU DON'T UNDERSTAND. I'VE MET SOMEONE. HE...
...HE **LIKES ME**.
LIKES YOU? PLEASE, RAPUNZEL! THIS IS WHY HE'S HERE, THE **ONLY** REASON.
GIVE IT TO HIM! GO AND **TEST** HIM... AND YOU'LL SEE.
WILL SHE HAVE THE COURAGE TO TEST EUGENE?
FOR NOW, RAPUNZEL HAS NO ANSWER. FOR NOW, SHE WILL HIDE THE SATCHEL.

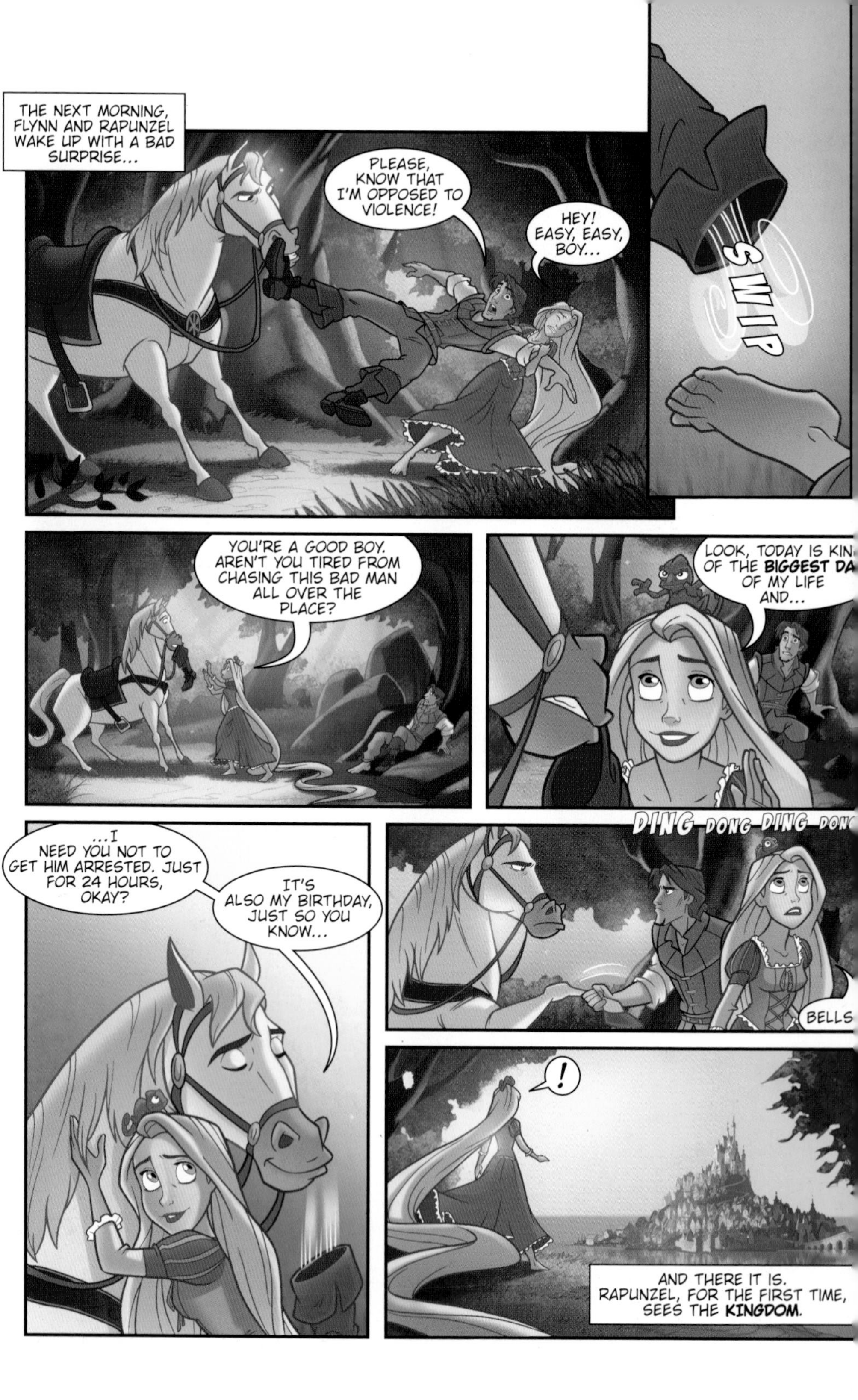
THE NEXT MORNING, FLYNN AND RAPUNZEL WAKE UP WITH A BAD SURPRISE...
PLEASE, KNOW THAT I'M OPPOSED TO VIOLENCE!
HEY! EASY, EASY, BOY...
SWIP
YOU'RE A GOOD BOY. AREN'T YOU TIRED FROM CHASING THIS BAD MAN ALL OVER THE PLACE?
LOOK, TODAY IS KIN OF THE **BIGGEST DA** OF MY LIFE AND...
...I NEED YOU NOT TO GET HIM ARRESTED. JUST FOR 24 HOURS, OKAY?
IT'S ALSO MY BIRTHDAY, JUST SO YOU KNOW...
DING DONG DING DONG
BELLS
!
AND THERE IT IS. RAPUNZEL, FOR THE FIRST TIME, SEES THE **KINGDOM**.

LATER, A PERFECT DAY BEGINS...

KINGDOM FLAGS!

THANK YOU!

...A DAY OF CELEBRATION IN THE KINGDOM...

...WHERE THE INHABITANTS MAKE RAPUNZEL FEEL AT HOME...

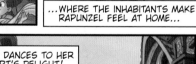

...SHE EXPERIENCES MYSTERIOUS EMOTIONS...

...AND DANCES TO HER HEART'S DELIGHT!

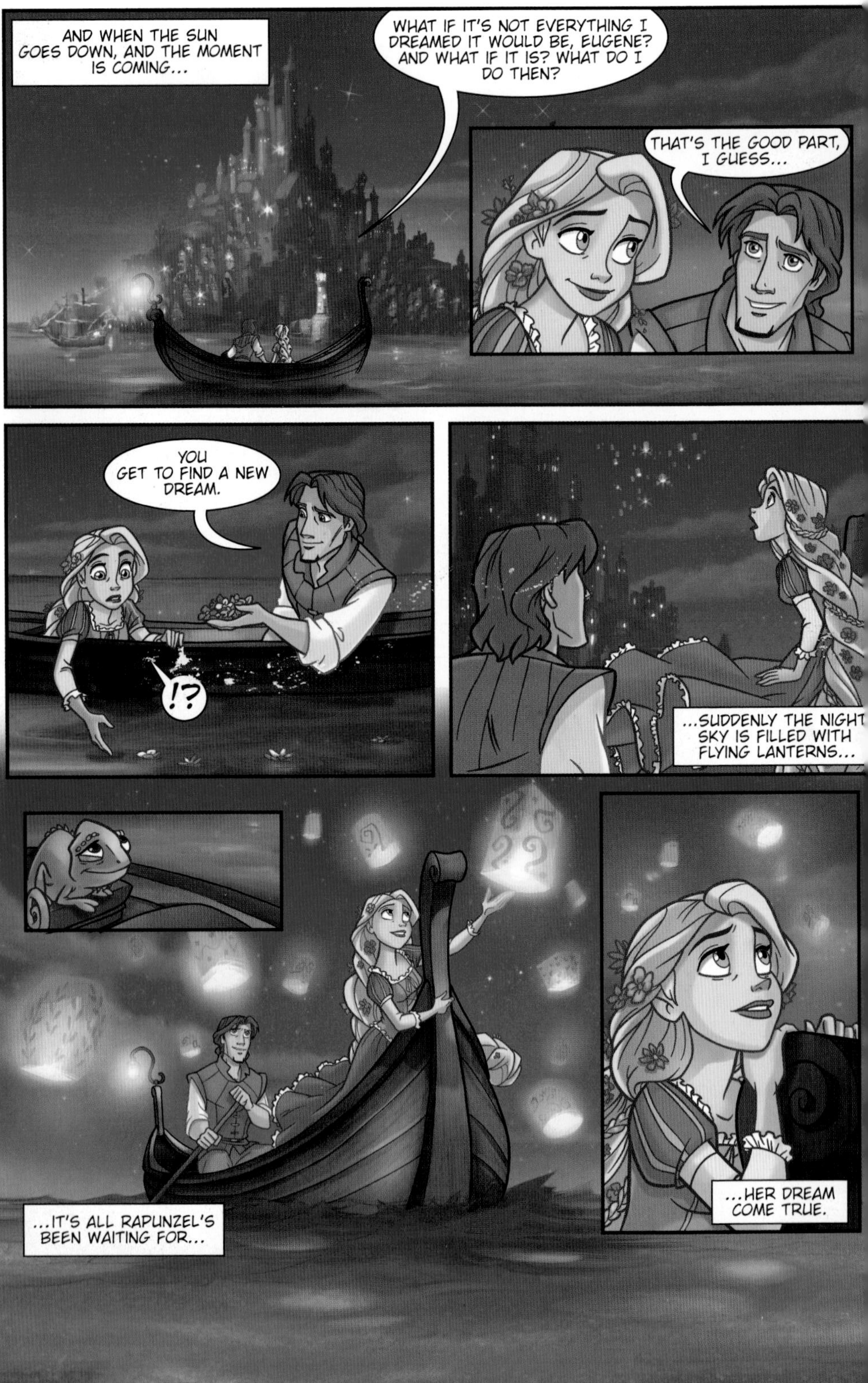
AND WHEN THE SUN GOES DOWN, AND THE MOMENT IS COMING...
WHAT IF IT'S NOT EVERYTHING I DREAMED IT WOULD BE, EUGENE? AND WHAT IF IT IS? WHAT DO I DO THEN?
THAT'S THE GOOD PART, I GUESS...
YOU GET TO FIND A NEW DREAM.
!?
...SUDDENLY THE NIGHT SKY IS FILLED WITH FLYING LANTERNS...
...IT'S ALL RAPUNZEL'S BEEN WAITING FOR...
...HER DREAM COME TRUE.

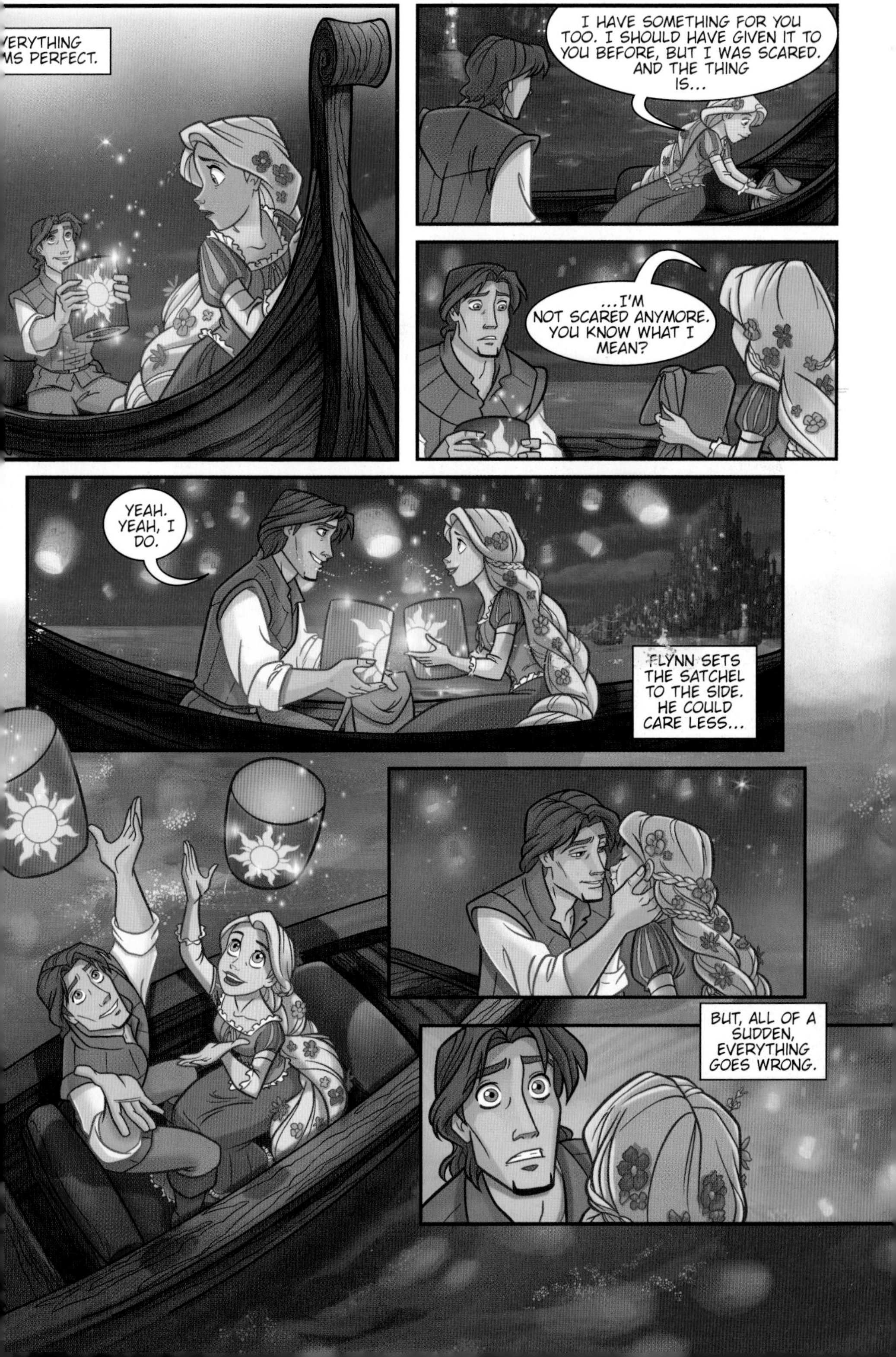

ERYTHING MS PERFECT.
I HAVE SOMETHING FOR YOU TOO. I SHOULD HAVE GIVEN IT TO YOU BEFORE, BUT I WAS SCARED. AND THE THING IS...
...I'M NOT SCARED ANYMORE. YOU KNOW WHAT I MEAN?
YEAH. YEAH, I DO.
FLYNN SETS THE SATCHEL TO THE SIDE. HE COULD CARE LESS...
BUT, ALL OF A SUDDEN, EVERYTHING GOES WRONG.

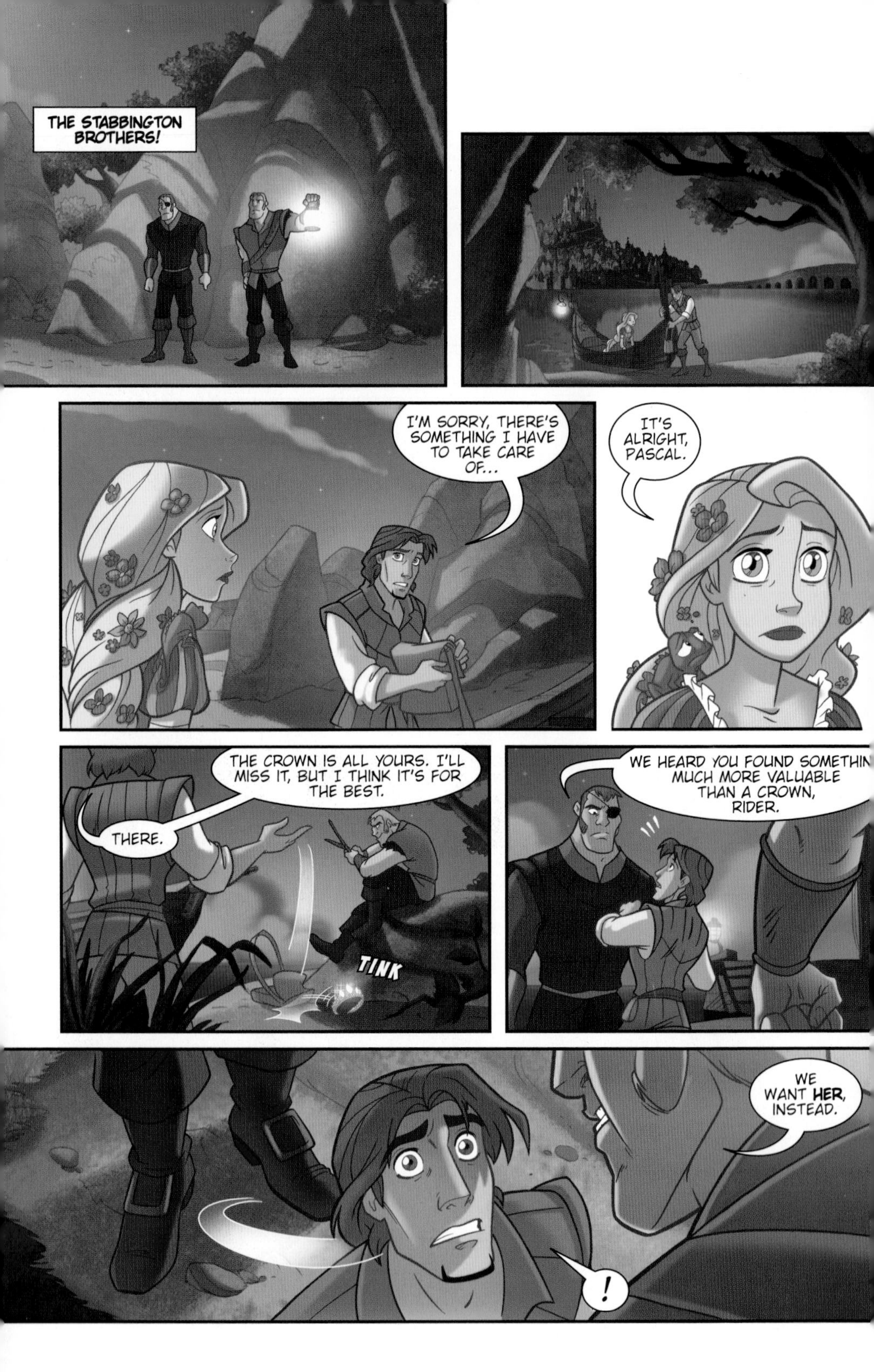
THE STABBINGTON BROTHERS!
I'M SORRY, THERE'S SOMETHING I HAVE TO TAKE CARE OF...
IT'S ALRIGHT, PASCAL.
THE CROWN IS ALL YOURS. I'LL MISS IT, BUT I THINK IT'S FOR THE BEST.
THERE.
TINK
WE HEARD YOU FOUND SOMETHIN
MUCH MORE VALUABLE THAN A CROWN, RIDER.
WE WANT HER, INSTEAD.
!

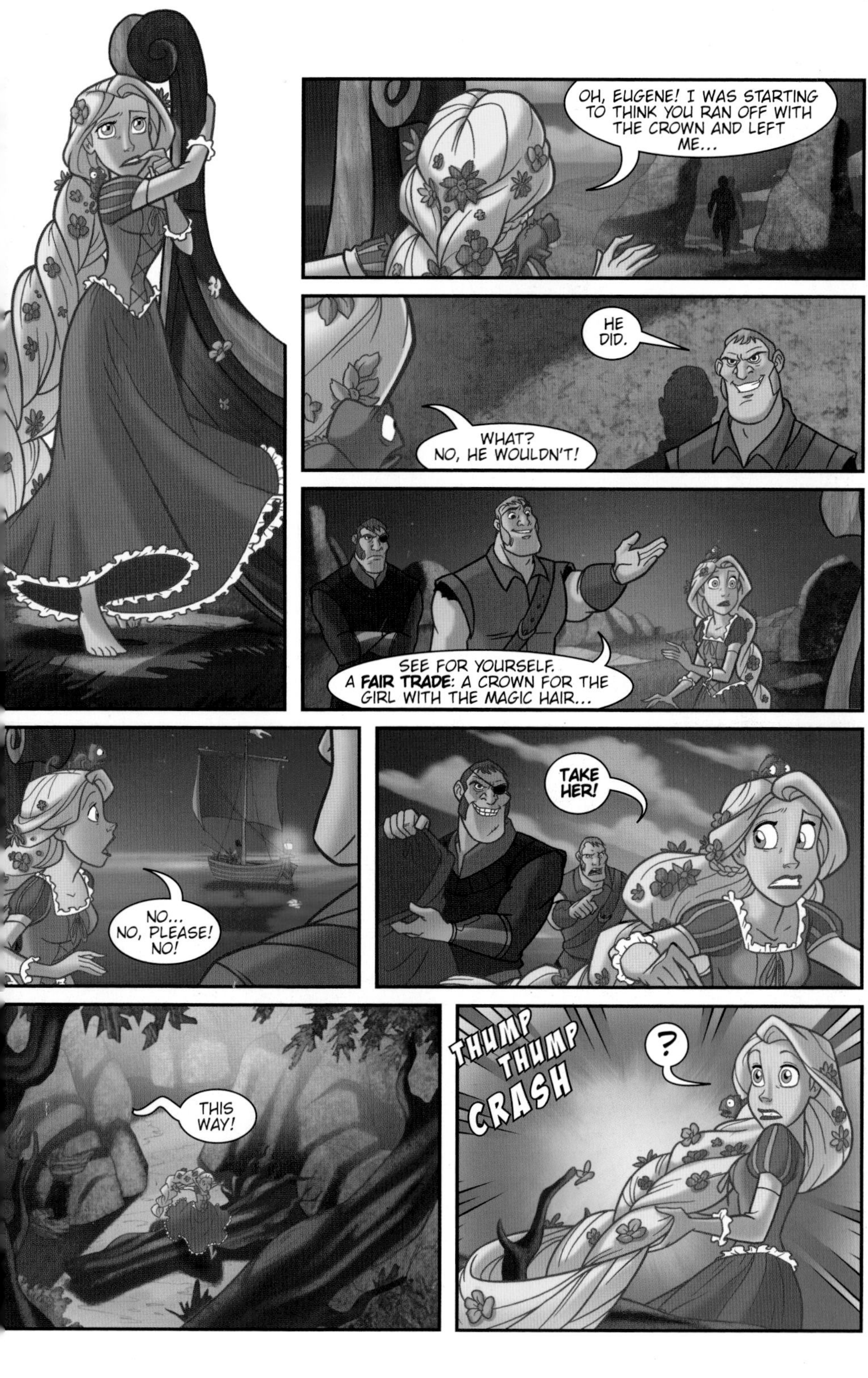

OH, EUGENE! I WAS STARTING TO THINK YOU RAN OFF WITH THE CROWN AND LEFT ME...
HE DID.
WHAT? NO, HE WOULDN'T!
SEE FOR YOURSELF. A **FAIR TRADE**: A CROWN FOR THE GIRL WITH THE MAGIC HAIR...
NO... NO, PLEASE! NO!
TAKE HER!
THIS WAY!
THUMP THUMP CRASH
?

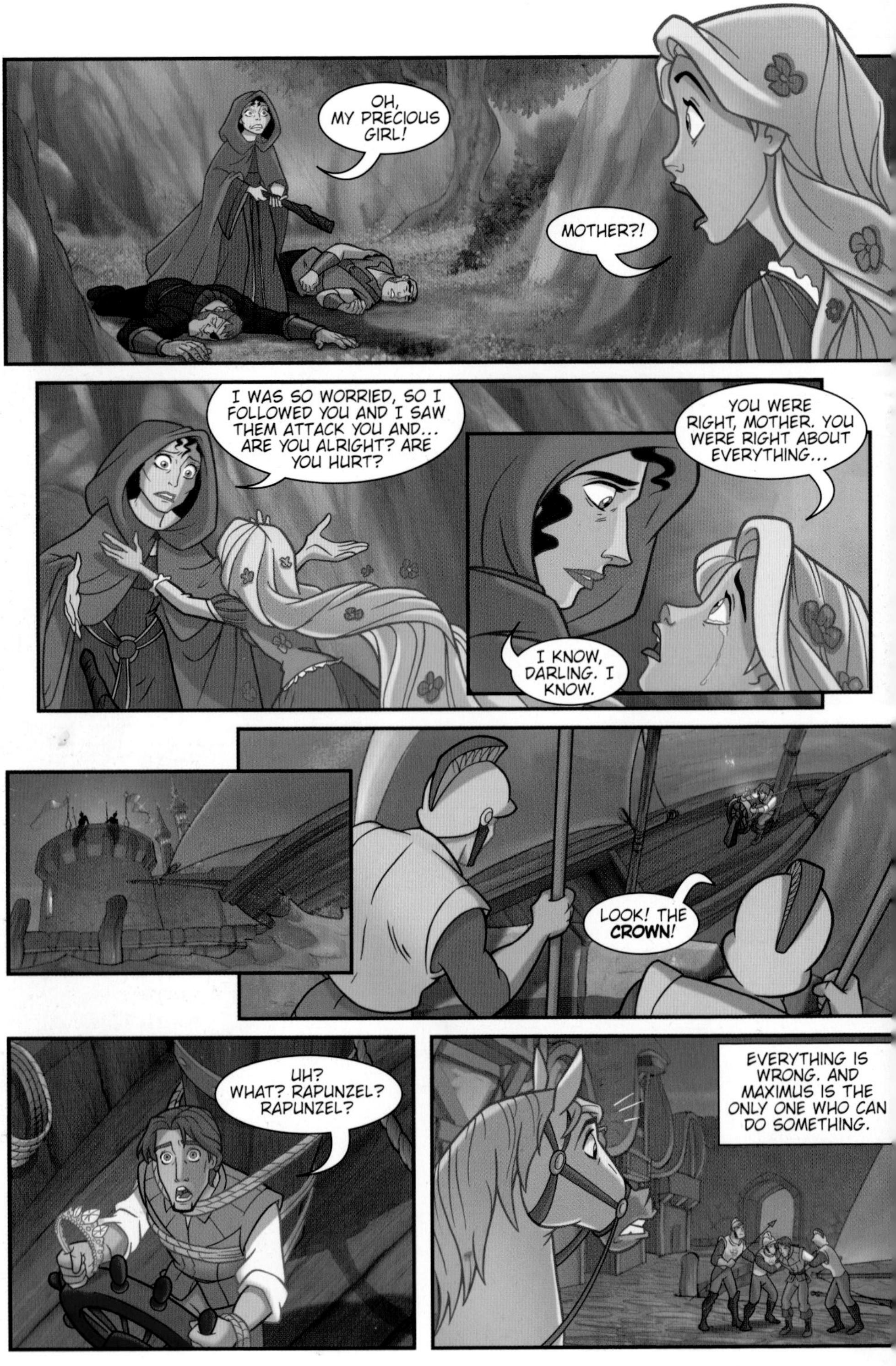
OH, MY PRECIOUS GIRL!
MOTHER?!
I WAS SO WORRIED, SO I FOLLOWED YOU AND I SAW THEM ATTACK YOU AND... ARE YOU ALRIGHT? ARE YOU HURT?
YOU WERE RIGHT, MOTHER. YOU WERE RIGHT ABOUT EVERYTHING...
I KNOW, DARLING. I KNOW.
LOOK! THE CROWN!
UH? WHAT? RAPUNZEL? RAPUNZEL?
EVERYTHING IS WRONG. AND MAXIMUS IS THE ONLY ONE WHO CAN DO SOMETHING.

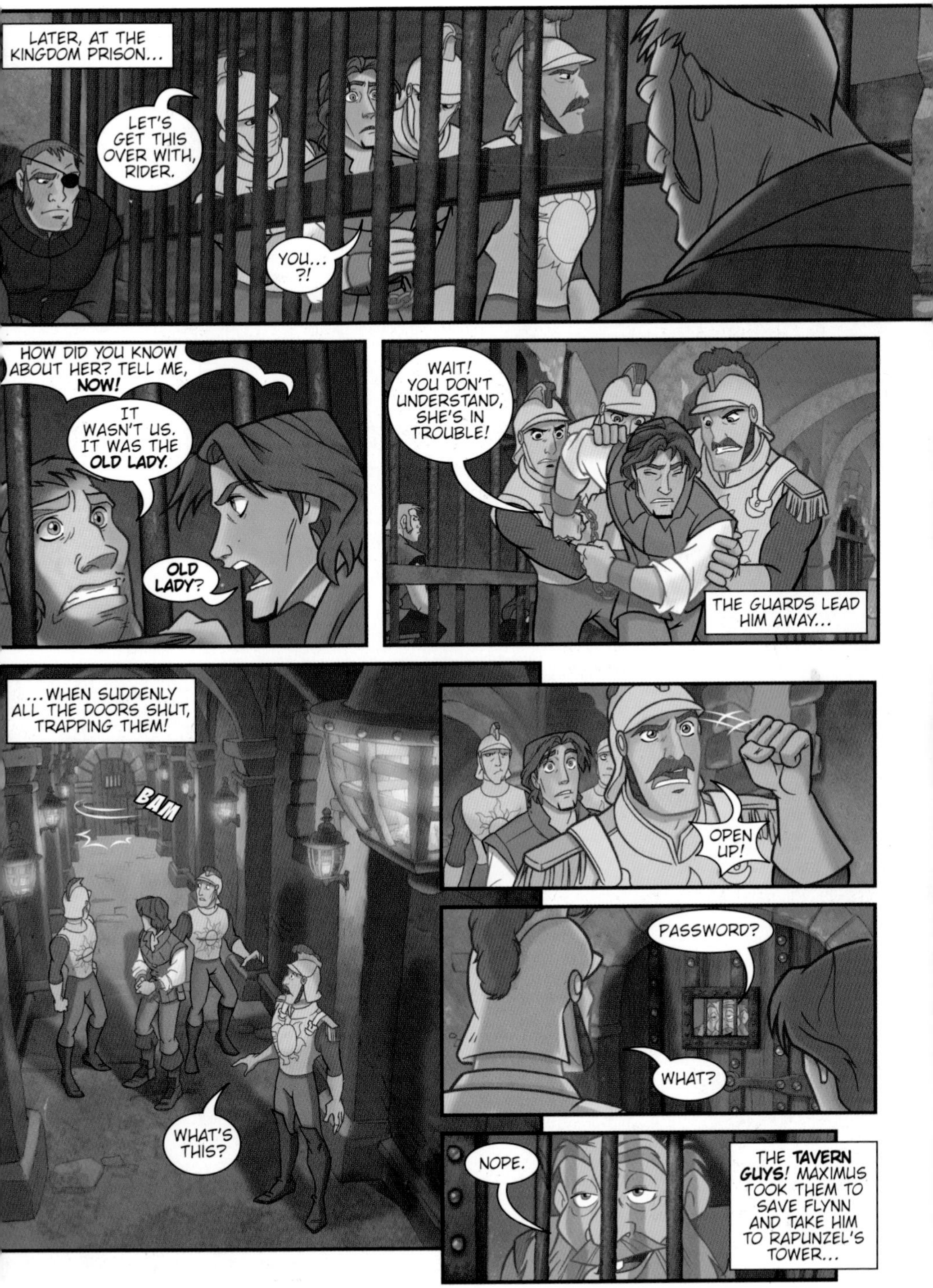
LATER, AT THE KINGDOM PRISON...
LET'S GET THIS OVER WITH, RIDER.
YOU... ?!
HOW DID YOU KNOW ABOUT HER? TELL ME, **NOW!**
IT WASN'T US. IT WAS THE **OLD LADY.**
OLD LADY?
WAIT! YOU DON'T UNDERSTAND, SHE'S IN TROUBLE!
THE GUARDS LEAD HIM AWAY...
...WHEN SUDDENLY ALL THE DOORS SHUT, TRAPPING THEM!
BAM
WHAT'S THIS?
OPEN UP!
PASSWORD?
WHAT?
NOPE.
THE **TAVERN GUYS**! MAXIMUS TOOK THEM TO SAVE FLYNN AND TAKE HIM TO RAPUNZEL'S TOWER...

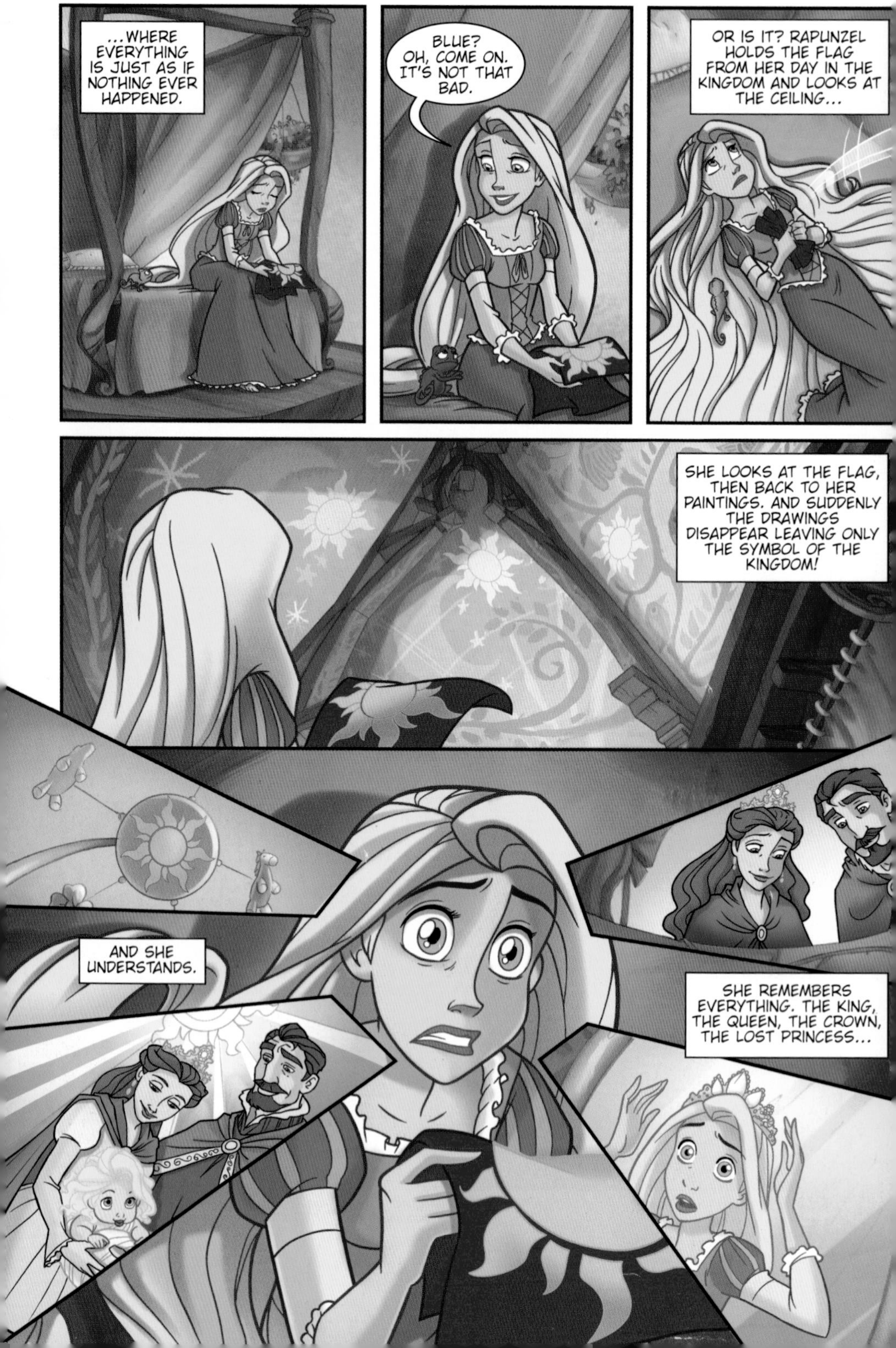
...WHERE EVERYTHING IS JUST AS IF NOTHING EVER HAPPENED.
BLUE? OH, COME ON. IT'S NOT THAT BAD.
OR IS IT? RAPUNZEL HOLDS THE FLAG FROM HER DAY IN THE KINGDOM AND LOOKS AT THE CEILING...
SHE LOOKS AT THE FLAG, THEN BACK TO HER PAINTINGS. AND SUDDENLY THE DRAWINGS DISAPPEAR LEAVING ONLY THE SYMBOL OF THE KINGDOM!
AND SHE UNDERSTANDS.
SHE REMEMBERS EVERYTHING. THE KING, THE QUEEN, THE CROWN, THE LOST PRINCESS...

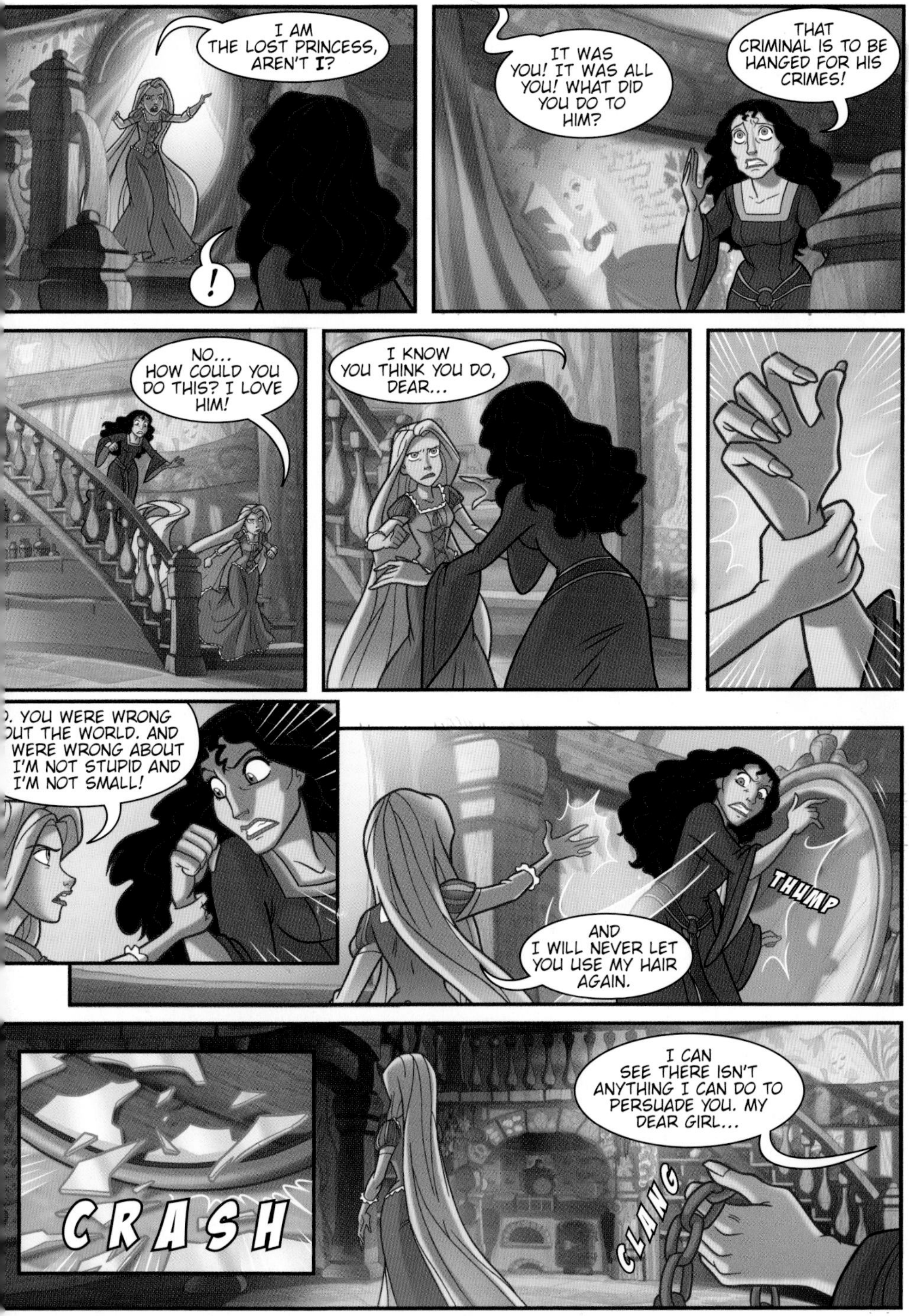
I AM THE LOST PRINCESS, AREN'T I?
!
IT WAS YOU! IT WAS ALL YOU! WHAT DID YOU DO TO HIM?
THAT CRIMINAL IS TO BE HANGED FOR HIS CRIMES!
NO... HOW COULD YOU DO THIS? I LOVE HIM!
I KNOW YOU THINK YOU DO, DEAR...
. YOU WERE WRONG
OUT THE WORLD. AND
WERE WRONG ABOUT
I'M NOT STUPID AND
I'M NOT SMALL!
THUMP
AND I WILL NEVER LET YOU USE MY HAIR AGAIN.
CRASH
I CAN SEE THERE ISN'T ANYTHING I CAN DO TO PERSUADE YOU. MY DEAR GIRL...
CLANG

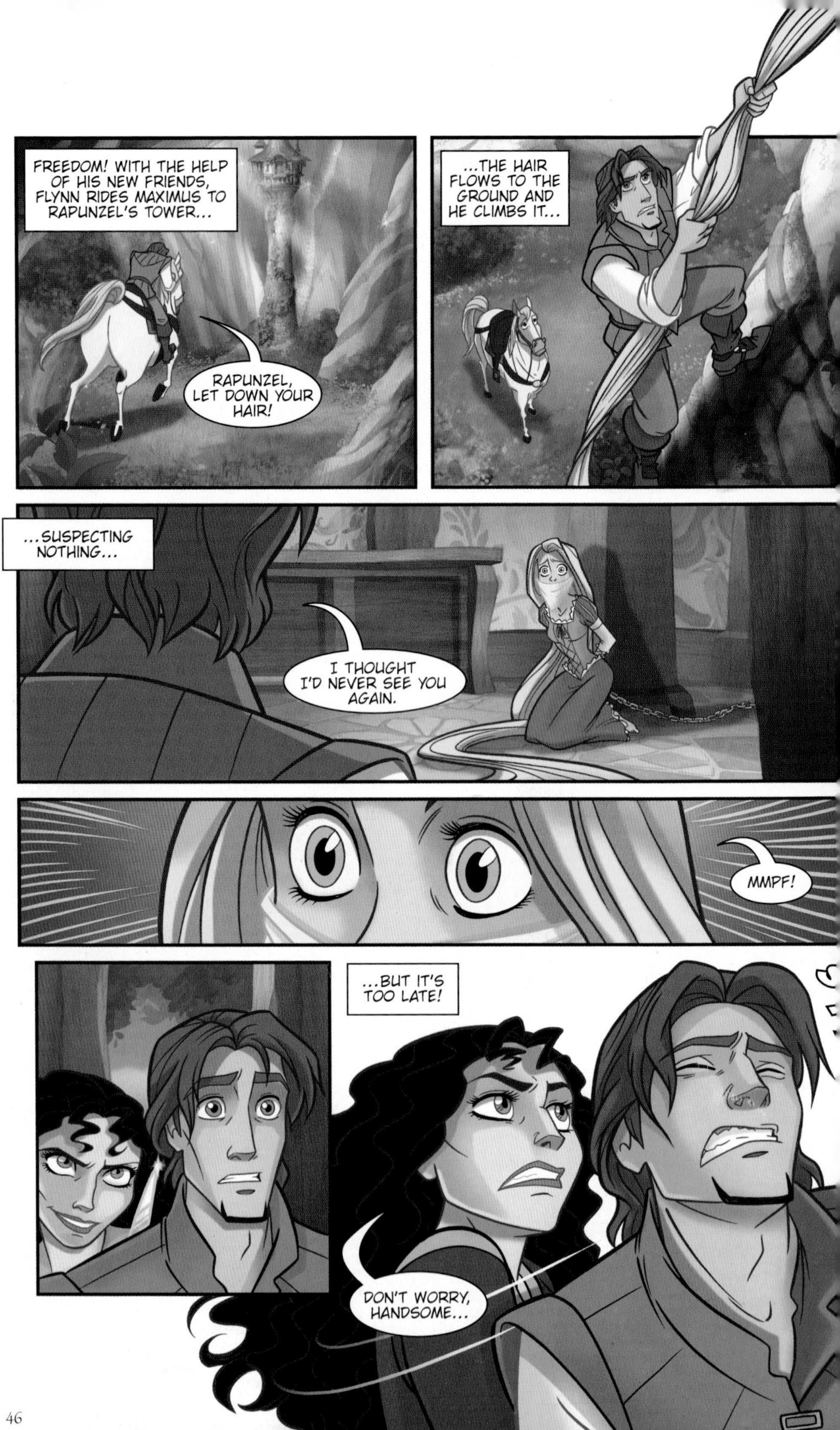
FREEDOM! WITH THE HELP OF HIS NEW FRIENDS, FLYNN RIDES MAXIMUS TO RAPUNZEL'S TOWER...
RAPUNZEL, LET DOWN YOUR HAIR!
...THE HAIR FLOWS TO THE GROUND AND HE CLIMBS IT...
...SUSPECTING NOTHING...
I THOUGHT I'D NEVER SEE YOU AGAIN.
MMPF!
...BUT IT'S TOO LATE!
DON'T WORRY, HANDSOME...

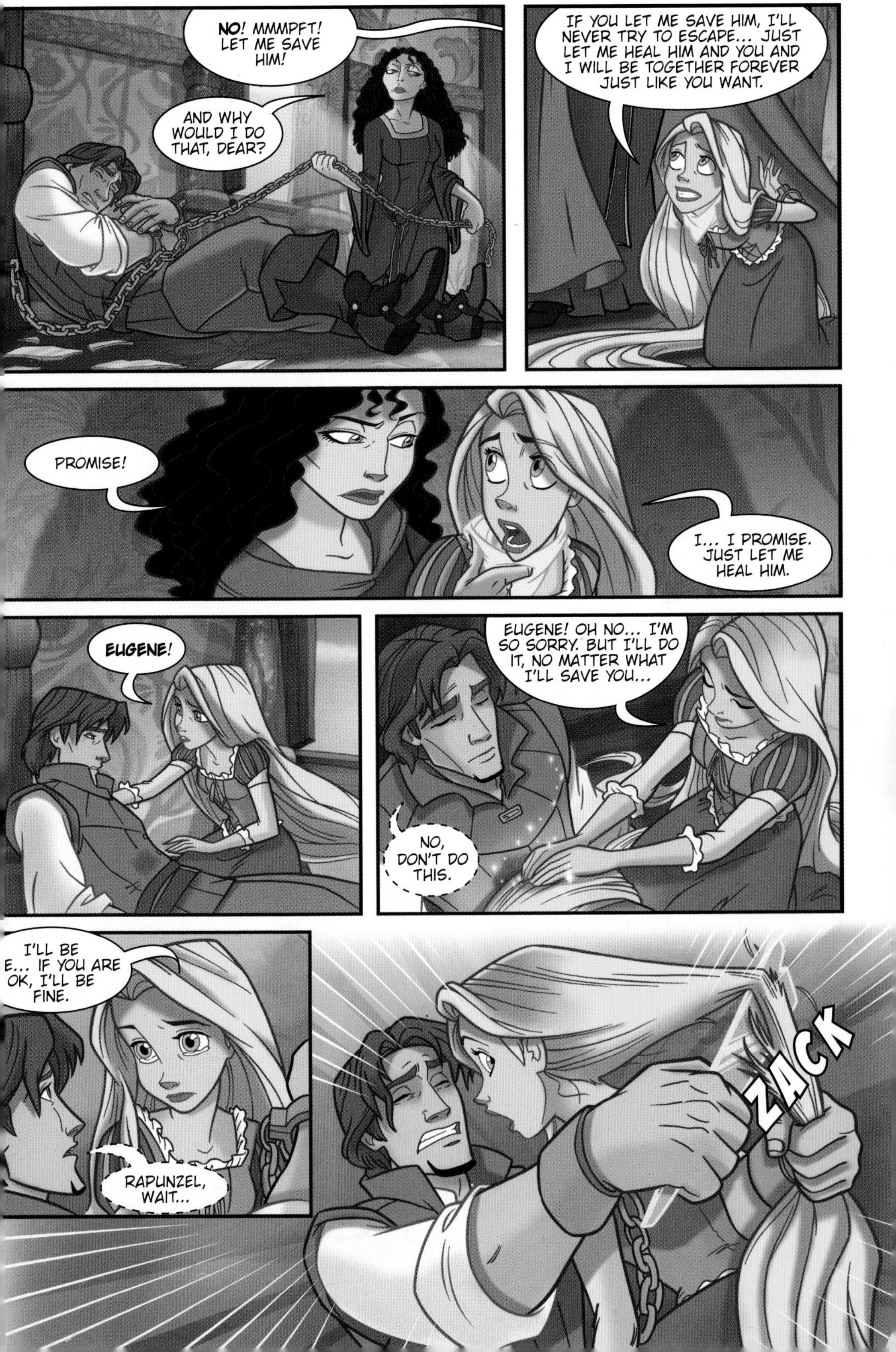
NO! MMMPFT! LET ME SAVE HIM!
AND WHY WOULD I DO THAT, DEAR?
IF YOU LET ME SAVE HIM, I'LL NEVER TRY TO ESCAPE... JUST LET ME HEAL HIM AND YOU AND I WILL BE TOGETHER FOREVER JUST LIKE YOU WANT.
PROMISE!
I... I PROMISE. JUST LET ME HEAL HIM.
EUGENE!
EUGENE! OH NO... I'M SO SORRY. BUT I'LL DO IT, NO MATTER WHAT I'LL SAVE YOU...
NO, DON'T DO THIS.
I'LL BE
E... IF YOU ARE OK, I'LL BE FINE.
RAPUNZEL, WAIT...
ZACK

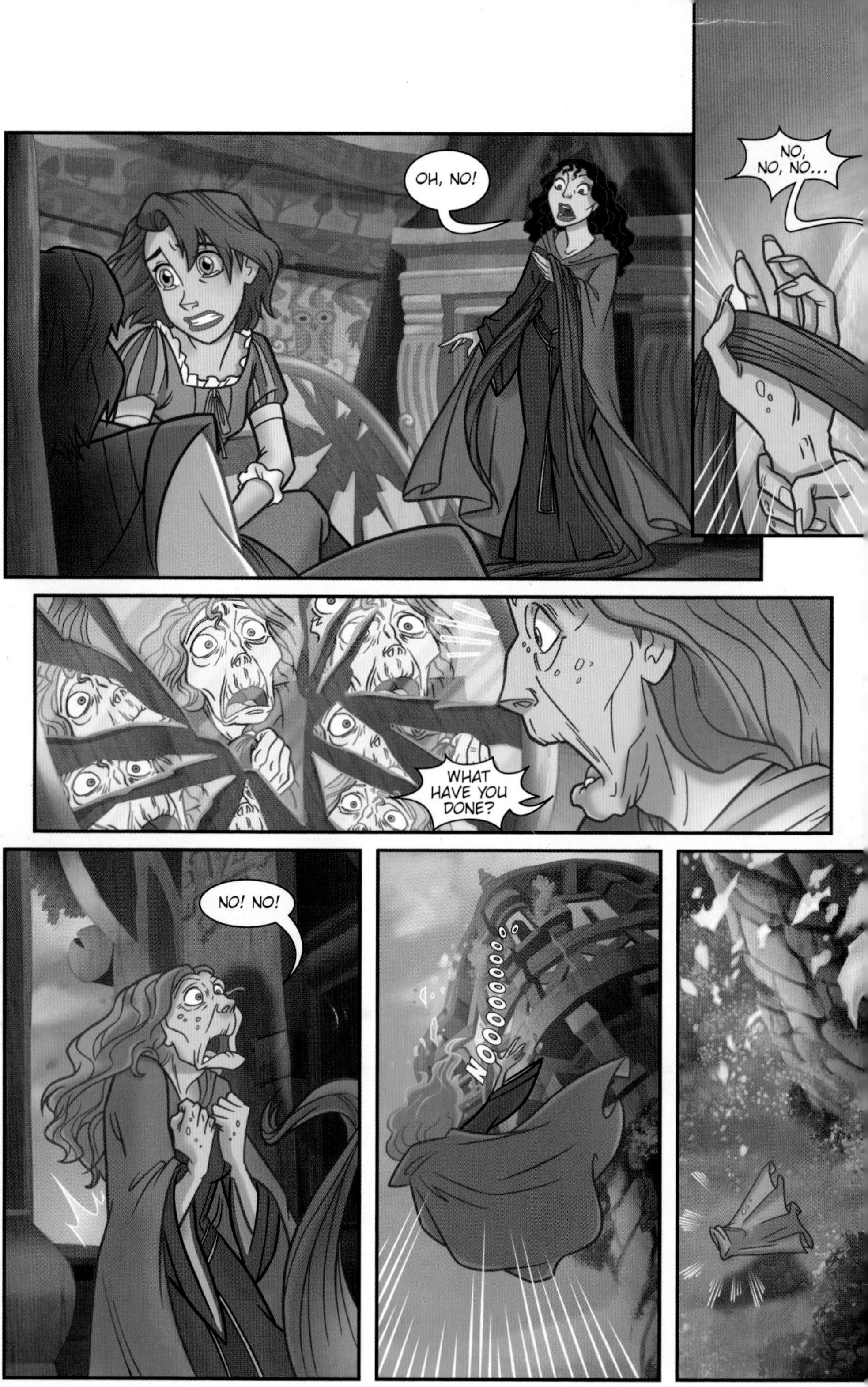
OH, NO!
NO, NO, NO...
WHAT HAVE YOU DONE?
NO! NO!
NOOOOOOOOOO

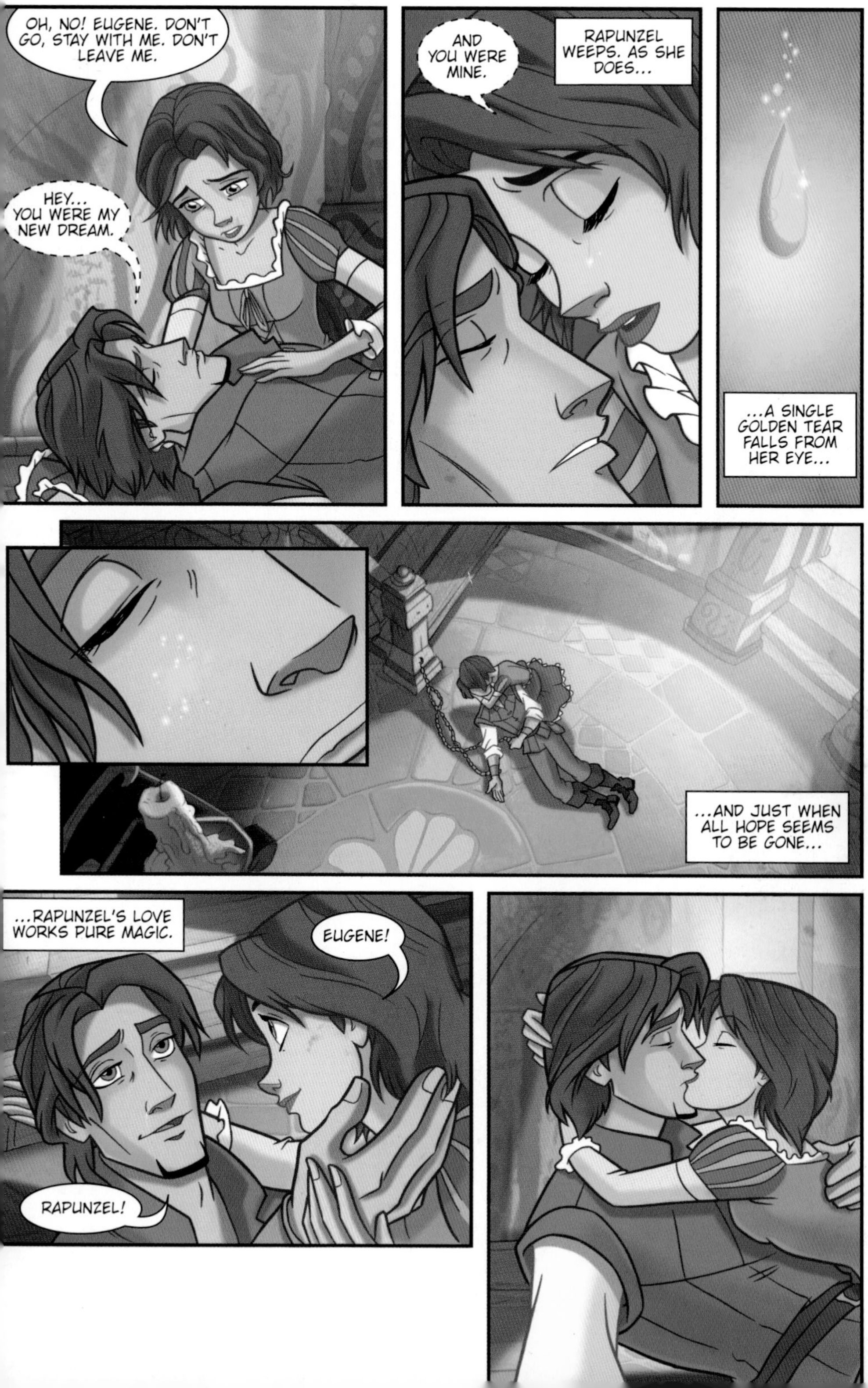
OH, NO! EUGENE. DON'T GO, STAY WITH ME. DON'T LEAVE ME.
HEY... YOU WERE MY NEW DREAM.
AND YOU WERE MINE.
RAPUNZEL WEEPS. AS SHE DOES...
...A SINGLE GOLDEN TEAR FALLS FROM HER EYE...
...AND JUST WHEN ALL HOPE SEEMS TO BE GONE...
...RAPUNZEL'S LOVE WORKS PURE MAGIC.
EUGENE!
RAPUNZEL!

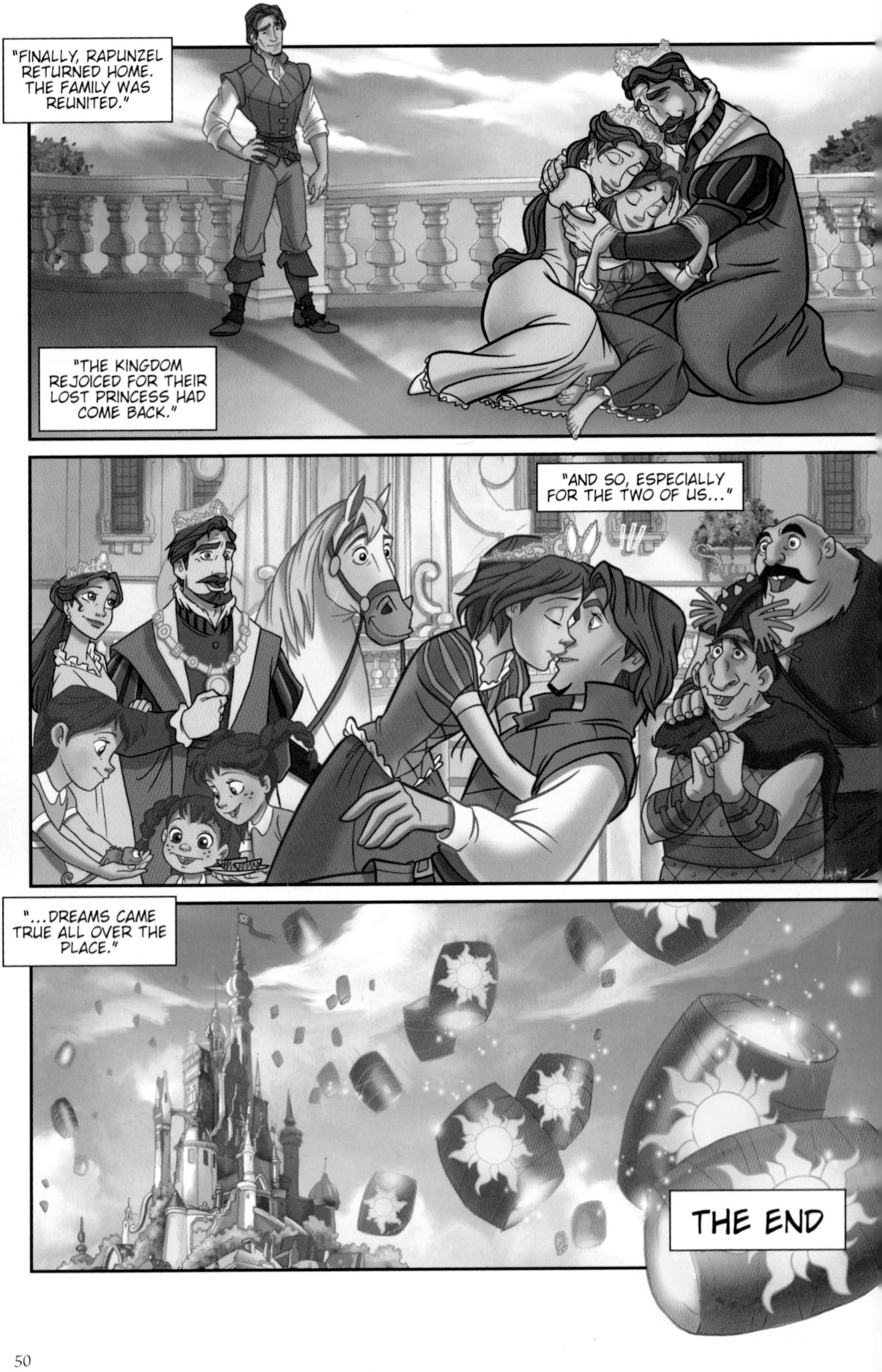
"FINALLY, RAPUNZEL RETURNED HOME. THE FAMILY WAS REUNITED."
"THE KINGDOM REJOICED FOR THEIR LOST PRINCESS HAD COME BACK."
"AND SO, ESPECIALLY FOR THE TWO OF US..."
"...DREAMS CAME TRUE ALL OVER THE PLACE."
THE END

Manuscript Adaptation
Alessandro Ferrari

Layouts
Elisabetta Melaranci

Clean-up (Characters)
Elisabetta Melaranci

Clean-up (Backgrounds)
Emilio Grasso
Luca Usai

Inks
Cristina Giorgilli
Francesco Abrignani

Paints
Angela Capolupo
Mara Damiani
Giuseppe Fontana

Paint Supervision
Stefano Attardi

Editing
Absink

Special thanks to Roy Conli, Nathan Greno, Byron Howard,
David Goetz, Katie Carter, and Renato Lattanzi

DARK HORSE BOOKS

President and Publisher **Mike Richardson**
Collection Editor **Freddye Miller**
Collection Assistant Editor **Judy Khuu**
Designer **Cary Grazzini**
Digital Art Technician **Samantha Hummer**

Neil Hankerson Executive Vice President • Tom Weddle Chief Financial Officer • Randy Stradley Vice President of Publishing • Nick McWhorter Chief Business Development Officer • Dale LaFountain Chief Information Officer • Matt Parkinson Vice President of Marketing • Vanessa Todd-Holmes Vice President of Production and Scheduling • Mark Bernardi Vice President of Book Trade and Digital Sales • Ken Lizzi General Counsel • Dave Marshall Editor in Chief Davey Estrada Editorial Director • Chris Warner Senior Books Editor • Cary Grazzini Director of Specialty Projects • Lia Ribacchi Art Director • Matt Dryer Director of Digital Art and Prepress • Michael Gombos Senior Director of Licensed Publications • Kari Yadro Director of Custom Programs Kari Torson Director of International Licensing • Sean Brice Director of Trade Sales

DISNEY PUBLISHING WORLDWIDE GLOBAL MAGAZINES, COMICS AND PARTWORKS

PUBLISHER Lynn Waggoner • EDITORIAL TEAM Bianca Coletti (Director, Magazines), Guido Frazzini (Director, Comics), Carlotta Quattrocolo (Executive Editor), Stefano Ambrosio (Executive Editor, New IP), Camilla Vedove (Senior Manager, Editorial Development), Behnoosh Khalili (Senior Editor), Julie Dorris (Senior Editor), Mina Riazi (Assistant Editor), Gabriela Capasso (Assistant Editor) • DESIGN Enrico Soave (Senior Designer) • ART Ken Shue (VP, Global Art), Manny Mederos (Senior Illustration Manager, Comics and Magazines), Roberto Santillo (Creative Director), Marco Ghiglione (Creative Manager), Stefano Attardi (Illustration Manager) • PORTFOLIO MANAGEMENT Olivia Ciancarelli (Director) • BUSINESS & MARKETING Mariantonietta Galla (Senior Manager, Franchise), Virpi Korhonen (Editorial Manager) • CONTRIBUTORS Elisa Checchi, Elisabetta Sedda, Bryce Vankooten

Published by Dark Horse Books
A division of Dark Horse Comics LLC
10956 SE Main Street
Milwaukie, OR 97222

DarkHorse.com

To find a comics shop in your area, visit comicshoplocator.com

First Dark Horse Books edition: February 2021
eBook ISBN 978-1-50671-750-0 | Hardcover ISBN 978-1-50671-741-8

1 3 5 7 9 10 8 6 4 2
Printed in China

Looking for Disney *Frozen*?

$10.99 each!

Disney
FROZEN
Breaking Boundaries

Disney Frozen: Breaking Boundaries
978-1-50671-051-8

Anna, Elsa, and friends have a quest to fulfill, mysteries to solve, and peace to restore!

Disney
FROZEN
Reunion Road

Disney Frozen: Reunion Road
978-1-50671-270-3

Elsa and Anna gather friends and family for an unforgettable trip to a harvest festival in the neighboring kingdom of Snoob!

Disney
FROZEN
The Hero Within

Disney Frozen: The Hero Within
978-1-50671-269-7

Anna, Elsa, Kristoff, Sven, Olaf, and new friend Hedda, deal with bullies and the harsh environment of the Forbidden Land!

Disney
FROZEN
Lead-up to the FROZEN II Story
True Treasure

Disney Frozen: True Treasure
978-1-50671-705-0

A lead-in story to Disney *Frozen 2.* Elsa and Anna embark on an adventure searching for clues to uncover a lost message from their mother.

Disney
FROZEN
ADVENTURES
Flurries of Fun

Disney Frozen Adventures: Flurries of Fun
978-1-50671-470-7

Disney
FROZEN
ADVENTURES
Snowy Stories

Disney Frozen Adventures: Snowy Stories
978-1-50671-471-4

Disney
FROZEN
ADVENTURES
Ice and Magic

Disney Frozen Adventures: Ice and Magic
978-1-50671-472-1

Collections of short comics stories expanding on the world of Disney *Frozen*!

AVAILABLE AT YOUR LOCAL COMICS SHOP OR BOOKSTORE!
TO FIND A COMICS SHOP IN YOUR AREA, VISIT COMICSHOPLOCATOR.COM

For more information or to order direct, visit DarkHorse.com

The classic tale of
Snow White and the Seven Dwarfs
reawakens!

Relive the beloved Disney fairy tale through the
first-person perspective of Snow White herself!

978-1-50671-462-2 • $12.99

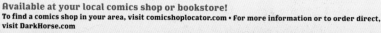

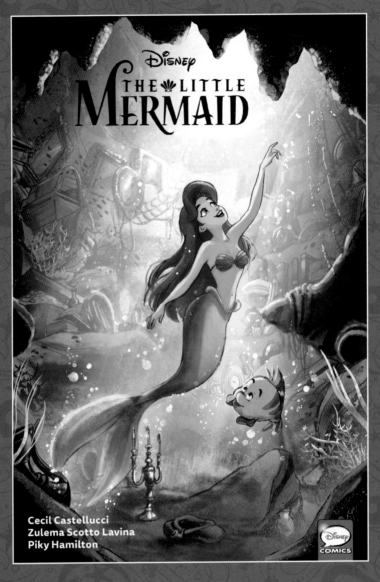